Wait On The Lord, I Say Wait

Sabriena Williams

ISBN: 978-0-9815463-8-4

This is a work of fiction. While, as in all fiction, the literary perceptions and insights are based on experience, all names, characters, places and incidents are either products of the author's imagination or are used fictitiously. No reference to any real person is intended or should be inferred.

All scriptural references taken from the
King James Version of the Bible

Editor:
Sharlyne Thomas

Proofreader:
Loretta Fuller

Front Cover Design:
Aidana WillowRaven
WillowRaven Illustration & Design Plus

Interior Design & Layout & Cover Layout:
Tarsha L. Campbell

Published by:
DOMINIONHOUSE
Publishing & Design
P.O. Box 681938 Orlando, Florida 32868
407.880.5790 phone
www.mydominionhouse.com

****

The Lord gave the word: great was the company of those that published it. (Psalm 68:11)

DEDICATION AND ACKNOWLEDGMENTS

This book is dedicated to my Godmother, Clinnie Mae Price. I know you are now with the Lord but I just had to say thank you. I want to personally thank you for being a light for me during my time of darkness. Thank you for not allowing me to wallow in doubt, guilt and shame. I thank you for not allowing me to have pity parties when I thought all hope was gone. I thank you for inviting me into your family and calling me daughter. I want to thank your children, Carolyn, Annette, Leon, Angela, and Cynthia for sharing you with me.

I also would like to personally thank James and Carmelitta Sheppard for being such a positive influence in the lives of Ja'kya and Je'rod as we traveled through our tough seasons. Your thoughtfulness and generosity meant a lot to me. Even though I did not say it often, I want to take the opportunity now to say thank you for all that you have done.

To my friends of faith: Stephanie McCray-Evans, Cynthia Davis, Carl Davis, Judith Martin, Barry McLeod, Calromea Ford, Carol Jones, Mr and Mrs. Kenneth Walker, Jennifer Taylor–Allen, Patrice Robinson, Vivian Rosas-Lee, Lavonda Larkin, Sheila Parker, Zeke Whitter, Sister Tammi Griffin, Toni Potter, Dee - Dee Wells, and Willie Mae Davis. Thank you all for believing in me when I wanted to throw in the towel. I love you all.

To my devoted readers, thank you for reading my book and sowing a seed into my ministry of writing. I love you and God bless.

Table of Contents

Wait on the LORD: be of good courage,
and he shall strengthen thine heart:
wait, I say, on the LORD. Psalm 27:14

Had God sent this man to her? Shavon wondered as she tried to sleep. For over a year, she had been praying that God would send her a righteous, devoted husband. She was very specific with God, asking Him to send her a husband who wanted to be a servant in the kingdom of God, one who would love her for herself, and who wanted children – a man much like her father...

CHAPTER I

WHEN THE SAINTS GO MARCHING IN

It was 10:15 Sunday morning and Shavon realized that once again she had seriously overslept. She was furious; her alarm clock never rang. Of course, she didn't remember turning it off. All night she had tossed and turned, guiltily thinking about the man she had met a few months ago online at Christian Café.

She knew her parents, especially her father, would not approve of her chatting online with a complete stranger, but she couldn't resist; she'd never met anyone else who made her want to stay up most of the night. It must have been past three in the morning when she had finally fallen into a fitful sleep; no wonder she had overslept.

'Mr. Black Emperor,' he called himself online. Why had he chosen that name? she wondered. And what did his voice sound like?

Of course she wanted to know what he looked like, but she did her utmost to avoid thinking about that; she didn't want to give into lust as she had with Kenneth and didn't want to be reminded of that pain. No, it was better to just imagine his voice. Maybe he sounded like James Earl Jones bringing the King James Version of the New Testament alive with his deep, rich voice. Oh yes, let him sound like James Earl Jones, she mused.

Had God sent this man to her? Shavon wondered as she tried to sleep. For over a year, she had been praying that God would send her a righteous, devoted husband. She was very specific with God, asking Him to send her a husband who wanted to be a servant in the kingdom of God, one who would love her for herself, and who wanted children – a man much like her father. Oh sure, her mother said Daddy had plenty of flaws, but Shavon could never see them.

But now she had to worry about being late for morning worship service for the third time this month. She didn't want to face Sister Karen's disapproving stare or have to put up with one of her scratchy, irritating speeches that usually went something like, "The Lord likes things done decently and in order and, Shavon, you being late to church is not according to the will of God." Now she had to rush. No luxurious milk and honey bath this morning, just a 'slap shower' – a slap of water here, another there, and that was it.

She felt good, energized, as if she were experiencing a kind of heady freedom, yet she knew that many would not approve of her chatting with Mr. Black Emperor, so it was also confusing. She smiled to herself. "Lord you said that everything we needed to know was in the word, so where can I find a verse on chatting with a man online?" She laughed lightly. Yes, she thought, I will need to pray about this for some guidance.

Quickly she picked out the magenta-colored suit she had bought at Macy's two weeks prior and the gold shoes that she had worn to work on Friday and that were still by the door where she had kicked them off. She stopped briefly to look in the full-length mirror. She looked surprisingly good despite very little rest. Quickly she grabbed her makeup, her purse and her bible and ran for the door like a football receiver running into the end zone for a touchdown.

"Here I come, Sister Karen," she said as she jumped into her beloved Mercedes 230I, gunned the engine, and set the air conditioning. Shavon sometimes thought that Sister Karen was a decoy from her parents to see if she was still obeying her elders as they had instructed her as a small child. Shavon could hear her mother's soft, sweet voice saying, "My little Vonny, honor thy father and mother so that you may live long in the land the Lord your God is giving you." Shavon knew that verse by heart; she had to recite Exodus 20:12 every time her parents thought she was being disobedient.

Shavon's father would say, "If you want to live a long prosperous life, then do what grown folks tell you; you hear me, Vonny?" In grade school, Shavon could never understand why her classmates would sass off to the teacher and say, "You ain't my mama. You can't tell me what to do!" All her life, Shavon had treated adults with respect, at least until now. She was going to respect Sister Karen even if she didn't feel she was due the wrath that was certainly awaiting her if she was indeed going to be late.

How old was Sister Karen? Shavon wondered. It was hard to figure out; but judging by the way she dressed, she was probably in her late sixties. All those boring polyester pant suits and dresses with matching scarves and black patent leather shoes. Shavon couldn't stand polyester and recalled how her Aunt Peggy used to order two-piece polyester suits from the Fingerhut Catalog and have them shipped to her parents' house because Uncle Dean used to get mad about her buying so many clothes on their fixed income. When she would arrive to pick up the package, she used to model the clothes for Shavon who couldn't understand why anyone would want to wear pants that had a permanent crease in them or why the fabric felt so coarse and lifeless. Yet Aunt Peggy was a spunky woman, she had the strut to prove it, and she always introduced herself as if she were a famous actress; so she could have worn much more interesting clothes to go with her detailed makeup.

"You look like Lena Horne," people used to tell her; and she would laugh and reply, "Honey, I wish I had the money Lena Horne has!" Aunt Peggy was so full of life and Shavon loved being around her.

When Shavon first joined the choir, Sister Karen tried to get the choir to collectively vote for and order coral two-piece polyester suits instead of choir robes. She was voted down, of course, because it was 2009 and no one wore polyester suits anymore except for her. Sister Karen had been the choir president at The Word Baptist Church for about 21 years and ran a tight ship, taking her role very seriously. She must have been a teacher in her younger days because she brought her black spiral attendance book to every rehearsal and took attendance name by name. If you did not say "present" quickly enough, she would mark you absent. "I will not tolerate tardiness," she announced frequently. "When the Lord comes back in the rapture, you better be ready or you will get left behind."

Rules, rules, rules! Sister Karen had a three strike rule: if you were late to choir rehearsal three times, you absolutely did not sing; if you were late to a singing engagement three times, you did not sing; if you were late, especially on the first Sunday of the month, you were definitely in the Devil's Pit! No gum, no giggling, and no talking while in the choir stand; and although everyone in the choir was at least twenty-one years old, most had a strong fear of Sister Karen.

Even her own daughter, Liz, was ordered to sit in the time-out pew one Sunday because she had been late three times to rehearsal. Liz tried to explain to her mother that she was delayed at work and had to pick up her dog from the vet, but her mother wasn't hearing any of it. You had to give Sister Karen credit: at least she made the rules apply to everyone. Shavon recalled one night when they were in rehearsal, Sister Karen said sternly, "If Pastor Dallas was in the choir and he was late, like he always is, I would sit him down, too! I'd make him preach from the floor." They all gasped at that thought. Would Sister Karen really do such a thing? Yes, she probably would.

Shavon drove as fast and safely as she could. "I'll make it; I'll make it," she repeated to herself for encouragement. The older, slower drivers were probably already in church, and the 'crazy' drivers wouldn't be on the road this time of morning – they're probably still at home nursing hangovers. The drive was made more pleasant with the help of local gospel station 1420 AM which featured a lot of the artists in the area each Sunday. Shavon enjoyed that although they often had problems with their frequency levels and occasional moments of total silence in the middle of a song. What Shavon was hoping for was her favorite song, "Psalms 23," by Juanita Bynum. From the first time she had heard that song at a wedding, Shavon knew it was a song she wanted to sing; and when Brother Detron introduced it to the choir, she knew it was the song for her. That song was so beautiful and she knew if she ever got an opportunity to sing it, she was going to have to do so with a willing heart and an open mind. And now that day was here – today she was going to sing "Psalms 23" during the morning service.

"Oh Lord," she muttered, "I haven't even practiced the song since Wednesday's choir rehearsal." Yes, she'd practiced alright! Sister Karen had made her sing her verses at least ten times. Brother Detron, who never said anything but didn't like the way Sister Karen often abused her authority, would not even give her eye contact – he just kept his head lowered toward the keyboard. By the time Shavon left choir rehearsal that night, she was severely hoarse and had to stop on the way home to get a large bag of lemons and a bottle of honey to make a soothing tea from a recipe Grandma Mamie had shown her when she had visited from the Carolinas with her bag of fresh herbs and abundance of home remedies. Grandma Mamie, known as a community nurse, was famous for helping the sick back to a full, clean bill of health with her home remedies

She remembered Grandma Mamie coming to visit in Florida when Uncle Joe, Daddy's younger brother, had become gravely ill. It was rumored that Uncle Joe had prostate cancer which was in its last stages. He'd lived a shattered and disjointed life after being discharged from the U.S. Military, and he used to always come on Sundays to see the family, but suddenly just stopped.

"He doesn't want to face us," Shavon's father explained. "He's ashamed of how he is living his life. He's fallen into doing things he ought not to be doing." Shavon watched her father religiously leave every Sunday with a plate of hot food, a few hygiene items, and a couple of dollars to give to Uncle Joe if he found him. By the time Grandma Mamie arrived in Florida, Uncle Joe had been given up for dead, but she removed him from the local hospital against the doctors' orders and brought him back to the house for 'treatment'.

Within ten days, Uncle Joe was up walking without his cane or walker; and when he went for his follow-up six weeks later, the doctors were completely amazed that the cancer was gone. Soon after, so was Uncle Joe who said that he didn't want to be a bother; he disappeared into the night like he had done so many times before. Shavon's father was deeply saddened; he prayed and asked God to protect his baby brother.

Thinking about family had caused Shavon's mind to drift, as it so often did, but now she saw that she had to change lanes to head toward the exit to the church. Just as she started to swerve, she saw the large green 15-passenger church van just ahead of her and narrowly avoided slamming into it. Trembling fiercely, she was switching lanes when, from the back of the van, a young boy of about seven years-old gave her the infamous finger. Shavon felt like she deserved it.

"Lord, I will accept what You allow," she said. "And Lord, please forgive that little boy and let the driver of that van know that I am really sorry for not paying attention."

Finally, she'd made it. As she approached the church parking lot, she could see cars wrapped all around the building. She'd forgotten Pastor Dallas' brother, Pastor Ruben B. Dallas, and his congregation were visiting today. There was not a single parking space in sight. She glared at the time on her dashboard console – she only had six minutes to park, get inside, put on her robe, compose herself, and be in line to march in with the rest of the choir without Sister Karen noticing she was late. Three times, she anxiously drove around the building but still no parking space in sight. But wait! She stopped at the vacant 'Pastor's Parking Only'. "Can I do it? Should I?" She glanced both ways as if she was about to steal the last cookie out of the jar – no one was watching. Swiftly, she whipped her car into the space and bolted for the entrance door as if she were superman trying to find a booth to change into his cape. She knew it was wrong to park in Pastor Dallas' parking space, but she figured she had plenty of time to move her car before he arrived. The joke around the church was that Pastor must have permanently programmed all his watches and clocks to be late because he never showed up to anything on time. Once when Shavon was in a stall in the children's bathroom, she overheard Sister Bernice say, "Girl, I don't care what anyone says. Pastor just wants to be seen, it ain't no way he is always late on accident." Sister Joyce replied, "You sho right, Sister Bernice. Remember when he was late for First Lady Dallas' mama's funeral?" Shavon had done everything within her power to not laugh because she knew the ladies didn't know she was there in the last stall. They were right – Pastor Dallas did make a grand entrance at that funeral after everyone had sat down. The doors of the church swung open and in pranced Pastor Dallas wearing a single-breasted rose-colored Versace suit, black Versace Oxford pointed-toe shoes, and to top off his attire, he was sporting grey-tinted unisex Versace sunglasses. These were the very same sunglasses Shavon had been trying to bargain hunt for because she couldn't afford a three hundred-dollar pair of sunglasses on her constricted budget.

With her heart racing, Shavon snuck through the children's church and ran to the choir robe closet, but her robe wasn't there. "Oh no! No!" Her palms were sweaty, her mouth was dry. Had Sister Brooks or Sister Cook picked it up for her when they realized that she was going to be late?

As she nervously made her way into the line, sure enough Sister Brooks handed Shavon her robe and gave her a wink. Shavon thought she had pulled it off; but when she zipped up her robe, the metal zipper made a loud piercing, screeching sound. Immediately Sister Karen swung her head in Shavon's direction, glared mightily, then rolled her eyes wildly.

Sheepishly, Shavon put her head down and prayed she wouldn't be written up in Sister Karen's 'Lamb's Book of Life'. As Sister Karen instructed the ushers to open the doors of the church, she gave Shavon another stern look for good measure. Brother Detron started the processional music and the choir took their positions around the altar for the congregational prayer.

When they started singing, Shavon lamented that she had to sing alto and furthermore, that she had to sing positioned between Sister Brooks and Sister Cook. Sister Brooks couldn't march because she wasn't coordinated and always forgot what foot to start on, so she always threw Shavon off until she ended up looking like she was marching to the beat of her own invisible drum somewhere behind her. As for Sister Cook, she couldn't hold a note if it was attached to a million dollars! She sang any note she felt like, it didn't matter to her, fluctuating between soprano and tenor and completely skipping alto. Sometimes she would even just speak the words instead of singing them. If you were in the congregation you might think she was the best singer in the choir because she used facial expressions and body movements which only made it that much worse to have to sing next to her. Marching between Sister Brooks and Sister Cook was like being led to the gas chamber – it was just that bad. Shavon snuck a look up at Brother Detron; his face told it all, but he just nodded in her direction and managed to suppress his laugh. Brother Detron knew Shavon's frustrations, but there was absolutely nothing he could do given that Sister Karen was in charge.

By the time the choir finally made it to the altar, Shavon felt as if she had just run a mile in the heat in the Baptist Choir Marathon! Throughout the hymn, Shavon kept her eyes on Brother Detron, knowing that if she made eye contact with anyone else, she was going to completely lose it. Brother Detron was hard to read, but she had a special connection with him. Just twenty-three years old, he led a very private life and spoke with very few in the choir. Sister Karen was always trying to introduce him to the single women; and while he was always cordial, he would say, "Thank you, Sister, but I'm way too involved with school and work to pursue a relationship right now." From Marietta, Georgia, he'd attended the local university on a music scholarship, completed his B.A. and was now working on his M.A. in music education. Before coming to The Word Baptist Church, he had played for several other churches part-time to supplement his income. An excellent musician, Brother Detron understood music inside-out; yet when Sister Karen would incorrectly insinuate that he was out of pitch, he just smiled and kept quiet to make her happy. One reason Brother Detron was probably submissive when it came to Sister Karen was because she was the one who had advocated that he be paid an annual salary instead of a weekly stipend, an honor he well deserved given that he was not only a skilled musician, but also deeply committed to the church and especially the choir. The word was that once he graduated, he would leave the Gator Nation area; so Sister Karen was doing everything within her power to keep him at the Church, even if it meant getting him married off to one of the single ladies.

After singing twelve stanzas of "When the Saints Go Marching In," Sister Karen motioned to the choir to stop singing and just hum the song quietly. The deacons were looking in the direction of the pulpit entrance door to see if Pastor Dallas would be making his grand 'late' entrance. But no, as usual Pastor Dallas didn't appear in time to conduct the congregational prayer. Deacon Smith made his way to the front of the church, cleared his throat, and asked the congregation to please bow their heads as he began to pray. His first prayer was for the Pastor and First Lady to arrive safely at the church. He then prayed for the church family, asking the Lord to let every family represented here today hear a word from God. He prayed for the drunks down on the corner, that God would take the taste from their mouth; he prayed for the men and women in prison. Deacon Smith's voice was fading in and out as the congregation interjected with, "Yes, Father. We need you, Father."

It was just as Deacon Smith started asking God to take care of the mosquitoes and ants that Pastor Dallas crept in, his brother in tow. Wearing a white suit, Pastor looked a bit like Casper the Friendly Ghost as he tiptoed to the pulpit, leaving his brother to take his place on the side. First Lady, dressed nicely as usual, was escorted to her seat by her armourbearer, Sister Carolyn. First Lady Dallas looked to be five to seven years younger than Pastor and wasn't a talker or one to socialize in large crowds, though she was always friendly in her own way. Shavon had once seen her at Macy's wearing jeans and a sweatshirt and looking a lot less tense then she usually did at church. That day she surprised Shavon by calling her out by name. Shavon was quite astonished. With The Word Baptist Church having over 1,500 members, it was pretty amazing that First Lady knew her name. To Shavon that was quite impressive, yet also a little suspicious. Why would she know her name?

Pastor Dallas approached the podium. "Good morning, Word Baptist Church."

"Good morning, Pastor Dallas," the congregation responded loudly. Yet they could all see that he was upset about something. He had a slightly bewildered look on his face and was speaking in a strangely grim tone of voice.

"God is good, isn't that right?" he asked.

"Yes, Pastor," the congregation replied.

For what seemed like forever, Pastor Dallas was totally silent and then said, "When God placed me as shepherd over this church, He instructed me to lead His people. He also told me to visit the sick, preach the word, teach the people and, as a leader, I hope I have gained the respect of my church family." "Lord, have mercy!" screamed women sitting on the "amen" pew.

"Lord, have mercy," Pastor Dallas continued. "If we call ourselves children of God, we have to let our actions speak louder than our words. We have to think like children of God, and our lights should shine all the time, not just when someone is watching. We have to be hearers and doers of His word. If we want to see Jesus, we must first see our neighbors and treat them right. We can't call Heaven our home when we can't get it right down here on earth."

Sister Brown stood up. "Amen! We got us a good Pastor. Give our Pastor some love."

The congregation began to shout, "Pastor we love you!"

Pastor Dallas looked about, nodded slowly, then removed his Bible from the podium and went to take his proper seat. Shavon didn't know what was going on but something wasn't right. And why did Sister Brown seem to be worshipping Pastor Dallas instead of the Lord?

"Sing, choir. Sing your praises," said Pastor Dallas.

As Brother Detron started playing the prelude to Shavon's song, she moved towards the microphone. She could feel someone looking at her but was too nervous to look up and see who it was. For a moment she froze; it had just dawned on her that she hadn't moved her car from Pastor Dallas' parking space – not much she could do about it now. She composed herself, cleared her throat, and began to sing. With her eyes closed, she pictured Jesus standing before her. She was dedicating this song to Him from her heart. Shavon could hear Sister Brown say, "Sing it Shavon, baby. Let the Lord use you. Hallelujah!"

So deeply moved by the spirit while singing, Shavon began to weep. Brother Detron immediately took over and the whole congregation was embraced by the presence of the Holy Spirit. Shavon found her way back to her seat with the help of Sister Brooks who whispered in her ear, "Baby, let the Lord use you." One thing Shavon loved about her church was that they didn't mind praising God; and when the Holy Spirit was present, the congregation let Him have His way. They were unabashedly enthusiastic in their love of the Lord.

When Pastor Dallas asked Sister Juanita Hill, the church clerk, to read the announcements, Shavon tried to remove her keys from her purse without making any noise. Sister Hill was an older woman who walked and talked on neutral, reading the announcements slowly with zero enthusiasm. Shavon had always thought that Sister Hill would make a wonderful funeral director given her lack of emotion. It didn't matter if was she reading a wedding or a funeral announcement, her droning tone never altered. This was Shavon's perfect chance; she could slip out and be back well before Sister Hill had finished the announcements. Miraculously, she was able to make it out without Sister Karen even noticing; but when she got to the parking spot, her car was not there! Instead, Pastor Dallas' pearl white Jaguar was sitting there on shining chrome rims and fourteen inch tires. Where was her car? She pressed her electronic car opener so that she could follow the sound – nothing. Fury rose up in her. Who had removed her car?

Seeing that the parking attendant was now there, she went over to him. "Excuse me, young man." She tried to keep her voice steady and friendly. "Did you see a black Mercedes that was parked in that space?" She pointed to the spot now occupied with Pastor Dallas' Jaguar. The parking attendant looked at Shavon as if she was speaking Hebrew and he didn't understand a word. She stood her ground.

"Yes," he finally responded. "Yes indeed, a black Mercedes was parked there; but upon the Pastor's request, it was towed to the garage across the street." He pointed in the direction of the garage, then walked to his security booth laughing hysterically while singing "When the Saints Go Marching In."

Shavon felt as hot as boiling fish grease! She could feel the steam rising from her head. Why had no one made a public announcement? She could have easily just gone out and moved her car. Of course, it was wrong for her to park where she had, but surely she hadn't deserved to have her car towed. There was nothing else to do so back inside she went. She tried to ignore the withering look from Sister Karen as she picked up her purse, but she did catch the shy wink from Brother Denton.

As she left the church, she could hear Pastor Dallas' brother, Pastor Rueben B. Dallas, state his topic for his sermon. "My topic this morning is 'Two Wrongs Don't Make a Right'." He spoke with boldness in his voice. "When someone has wronged you, march them before the Lord; tell the Lord about it. Don't try to fight your own battles. Vengeance is the Lord's, I say. Vengeance is the Lord's." Shavon wondered if maybe she should stay to hear what 'thus saith the Lord' about wrongs, but her hot flesh was getting the best of her and she needed to be sure her car and all her possessions inside of it were alright. She looked in the direction of the garage across the street. In the dead heat of summer and in heels, this was going to be penance enough. As she wobbled her way across the street, a thought entered her head: What if the garage was closed already? It was Sunday and not too many businesses stayed opened on Sundays.

"Oh please, please, let it be open," she prayed. No way would she be late for church again and run the risk of not finding a parking space. "I'll be on time from now on. I'll be obedient." Yes, she told herself, I've been taught a lesson by God and I won't forget it.

Two young men wearing oversized shorts and basketball jerseys lounged against a 1974 box-style Chevy Impala outside of Snoop's Garage and Towing Service. As Shavon got closer, she saw them putting out a blunt. One of them reminded her of Rodney, Sister Brown's youngest boy, who used to come to church with Sister Brown, but hadn't come for quite a while. This could very well be him, Shavon thought. The music blaring from the car was so loud that her eardrums trembled.

"Excuse me," Shavon said with caution, "but could you tell me who I need to see about a car that was towed here earlier today?"

"You have to see Snoop," replied one of them.

The young man that Shavon thought was Rodney chimed in. "You asking about that tight Mercedes that was brought in earlier?"

"Yes. That's the one," Shavon replied, pleased he liked her car. "Do you know where it is?"

"In the back. I saw Snoop take it back there." He appraised Shavon carefully. "I didn't know church ladies rolled like that. Fine car, those custom rims and all."

"Thank you. How do I claim it?" Shavon was not in the mood for pleasantries. She was hot, she was tired, and she was very, very hungry. It was only now that she realized she hadn't had any breakfast.

"Snoop's over there." The young man jerked his thumb in the direction of a store across the street. "You can wait here in the Chevy with the A/C or you can wait inside where there ain't no air." "I'll wait inside," Shavon said, and started toward the door of the office.

As tempting as the offer was to sit in the Chevy with the air conditioning on, she really didn't want to have to talk to them. "Man, I wouldn't mind having one of those church freaks," she heard as she opened the office door. She ignored it. "Lord, forgive them, for they know not what they say or do," she muttered.

The office was stifling and rap music played from a small radio. As always, Shavon noted that the lyrics were about killing and other obscenities. Why did people like this boisterous music? Deciding to make the best of this time, Shavon pulled her cell phone from her purse so she could call her best friend, Alana; but the battery flashed dangerously low, so she turned it off in case she might need to call 911. Just then the door opened and in walked a man covered in oil from his head to his feet, huffing and puffing as if he was having an asthma attack.

Shavon prayed silently, Oh Lord, please don't let this man have an asthma attack because I'm not sure I'd be able to perform C.P.R. on him if he collapses.

"I'm Snoop," said the man as he extended his hand. But as Shavon reached out to shake his hand, he jerked it back again as if just remembering how dirty and oily his hands were. He eyed her body up and down.

Shavon coughed and thought, what was it with the men in this garage? "Excuse me, Mr. Snoop, but I've come to collect my car."

Snoop dragged his eyes away from her body. "Yes. I've had your car for an hour," he chuckled. "You a new member of the church?"

"No, I've been a member for many years. Why?" And why was he laughing? she wanted to ask. Did he think this was funny?

"You aren't the only one this month," said Snoop. "Good ole' Pastor Dallas has a strict policy about parking in his space. I got a contract with the church to tow any car that's illegally parked."

Shavon wanted to march back across the street and give Pastor Dallas a piece of her mind from Genesis to Revelation. But vengeance is the Lord's, she reminded herself. And anyway he wouldn't be there; he never stuck around after service. He's better than the Great Houdini -- now you see him and now you don't, she thought and started to giggle.

"Wait here, ma'am," Snoop said. "I'll have one of those knuckleheads outside pull your car around for you."

"Thank you, sir," Shavon said, "but just tell me how much I owe you and where it is, and I'll be on my way." She didn't let anybody drive her car. She'd worked way too hard to let anyone rough ride it. She pulled out her credit card. "How much is it?"

Again Snoop chuckled. "Well, it's eighty five dollars. But, see, your Pastor has already paid it in full." Shavon breathed a sigh of relief. She made good money with the non-profit organization she worked for as a program operations director, but towing a vehicle wasn't in her budget for this month.

Out back, she saw her "baby" immediately. It was parked next to a 1986 Lincoln Town Car that had only three tires and had bullet holes all over the body. Shavon inspected her car with eyes that might have come from a hawk, everything seemed to be the way she left it. She opened her glove compartment and saw that her ATM card and checkbook were still in place. "I need to stop leaving them there," she told herself. Exhausted, she cranked up her car, turned on the air and drove through the gates as if they were the gates to freedom. Veering onto the highway, she laughed again. "Either God has a great sense of humor, or I have just been thoroughly tried. Or both!"

As tired as she was, she was not going to skip her Sunday ritual of treating herself to a dinner from June Bug's Soul Food Shack. She was now so hungry and thirsty that she had cotton mouth, but some of June Bug's lemon sweet tea was going to cure that in a little while. As she pulled into their parking lot, she knew she was going to be ordering with her nose. Just the smell of June Bug's menu items would send any person into a tail spin.

When her turn came, she ordered an oxtail dinner with extra gravy. It came with collard greens, yellow rice, candied yams, honey butter cornbread, and a slice of sour cream pound cake. Shavon was tempted to get another slice of cake, but she hadn't been to the gym in a few weeks so she fought the temptation.

As she waited for her order, she realized she hadn't even had time to think about Mr. Black Emperor all morning. Had he thought about her? she wondered, or had he done better than that and also gone to church?

Either would be fine, she said to herself, smiling.

One day, she thought maybe she and her Black Emperor could enjoy an early dinner there or even lunch after church one Sunday. Did he like soul food? she thought. Next to seafood, soul food was her favorite. It had been such a long time since Shavon had been on a date so even thinking about where she would go for a date was silly, but it would be a good place to go with Mr. Black Emperor...

CHAPTER II

ONE HECK OF A DAY

On the way home, Shavon could smell the scrumptious aroma from the food she had purchased from June Bug. She hated to admit it, but June Bug's food was better than her mother's Sunday cooking although she would never tell her mother that. One thing she knew for sure: you didn't insult a black mama about her cooking and still expect to get a hot meal once in a while.

The food was on the back seat so she wouldn't be tempted to eat her honey butter cornbread. She had a tendency to nibble it as she drove so that when she arrived home it would be finished. It was not just the food she liked about June Bug's café, it was also the Christian atmosphere. They always had gospel music playing in the background; and on some Sundays, featured soloists or church groups.

One day, she thought maybe she and her Black Emperor could enjoy an early dinner there or even lunch after church one Sunday. Did he like soul food? she thought. Next to seafood, soul food was her favorite. It had been such a long time since Shavon had been on a date so even thinking about where she would go for a date was silly, but it would be a good place to go with Mr. Black Emperor. She could introduce him to June Bug, the owner, who made sure all his customers felt welcome; he went out of his way to make you feel at home. Now and then he would come out of the kitchen to introduce himself to a new customer, and Shavon recalled the first time she laid eyes on June Bug. She was at the counter ordering a lemon sweet tea and an order of honey butter cornbread when a man came out of the kitchen singing loudly, "Cooling water; cooling water." She smiled as he walked toward her.

"Afternoon, Woman of God, how are you today?" he said cheerfully.

"I'm just fine, sir," she replied. "And how are you?"

June Bug was so tickled that Shavon called him sir that he said, "Woman of God, no need to call me sir, just call me June Bug. Everyone else in the family does, and you are family." He was short, stocky, and bald, but it was pretty clear that back in his younger days he was probably a stud. Now, it seems gravity and friction had taken over. His protruding abdomen resembled the belly of a seven months pregnant woman and was supported by very tiny legs. He always spoke in the loudest of tones and had a heavy southern accent, a man that Southerners might call a Gullah, and he was one of the friendliest restaurant owners Shavon had ever met.

All the way home, she looked forward to devouring her food. She thought about pinching off a corner of her honey butter cornbread when she paused at a red light but decided against it. No, she wanted to eat it all at once.

"One heck of a day." She smiled. What else could go wrong?

As she pulled into her driveway, she noticed that her front lawn grass was turning brown. She needed to call her yardman to find out what was going on; she didn't need a note from her homeowners association president, Mrs. Frost, about her discolored grass. Shavon had been to homeowners association meetings where they trashed other neighbors about their landscaping. She wanted to stay off the bad-neighbor list. Shavon looked at her front door before pulling into the garage and saw a large piece of paper stuck there.

"Well, that's it," she muttered. "Another thing gone wrong." The 'lawn police' had already been to her house. "What other lessons are You going to teach me today, Lord?" she asked.

Once inside, she tossed her purse and keys on the breakfast counter, kicked off her shoes, and went to the front door to see what was in store for her. Shavon rarely used her front door; the garage entrance was much easier. The note was taped to the door with a band-aid that was moist from the heat and barely hanging on. She didn't even have to open the note to know exactly who it was from: Mo'keisha, her ex - boyfriend Kenneth's first cousin. Mo, as Shavon called her, was the most ghetto person she knew. A resourceful young woman who knew how and where to get anything she wanted, Shavon had befriended her from the first day they met even though she knew that Mo was going to be a work in progress. A certified hustler, Mo had shown up at Shavon's house at least every other month on a Sunday for the last five years. She chose Sundays figuring that Shavon would be a bit more charitable after church. It was the ideal day to drop a sad story on Shavon.

"You got more stories than the dictionary has words," Shavon had once said to Mo. Again and again she talked to Mo about getting and keeping a job to provide for her three children; but Mo's philosophy was that if a man wanted to take care of her, she was going to let him. To her credit, Mo never tried to disrespect Shavon's beliefs about God; she said that she just didn't have the time for God to work miracles when she needed nail money or weave money. Her standard answer whenever Shavon talked with Mo about trusting God and inviting Him into her life was to explain that so many men in her life abused her, so why would she sell out her life for a Man she couldn't even see, touch, or talk to?

As a small child, Mo had been molested by her aunt's husband and then got pregnant when she was only fourteen years old. Her boyfriend had promised he was going to take care of her but left town never to be heard from again. Mo had to put the baby up for adoption; something she regretted to this day. From the time she had given up her child, Mo had lived a really promiscuous lifestyle, equating the attention that she received from men as love. Shavon knew that once Mo found out what real love was, her promiscuity would be over. She often prayed that God would heal Mo's heart from the pain she had endured from childhood until now as a young adult. She had three beautiful children and four 'baby daddies' and was convinced that two men fathered her youngest child, Tyra. "She got two DNAs," Mo insisted, "because she got two daddies." Her oldest son, Jaheem, was now eight years old and was born when Mo was eighteen. She was elated when she found out she was pregnant with Jaheem. She was going to keep this child; no way was she giving up this one. Mo had told Shavon how she walked around for nine months being teased by her friends about her baby being a bastard and would be forced to give this one up too because she was too poor to raise it alone. "Listen,

Vonny," Mo had said to Shavon, "I done some really bad things in my life, so why would God want to love me?"

"God forgives all," Shavon explained. "Your problem is that you won't forgive yourself. You need to love yourself."

"All that stuff about love," Mo stopped in mid-sentence, looking away for a moment. "Terrence said he loved me. He said he was never going to leave me and that he was going to get a decent job and get us a house and fancy cars and all. Then he ran off when I got pregnant and I was only fourteen. See, that is what I know about love. I still got letters he wrote me before I got knocked up; they talk about love. So don't go talking to me about no love 'cuz all I know is that love gets you hurt and lonely."

Jaheem's father had stuck around for a few years until he was incarcerated for strong-arm robbery. Mo tried to hang in there with him by visiting and writing; but since he could no longer lavish her with the things she wanted, she let him go. Before that, he used to pay her thirty-six-dollar Section 8 rent every month and would put wads of spending money in her pockets for her and the baby. It didn't matter to her that he had several other 'baby mamas' on the other side of town as long as he was taking care of her and her baby. She was happy at that time. She had a man who she thought loved her and her baby; so when her fairytale picture turned into a lifetime story, she was once again devastated. Her motto became that she wasn't about to be used anymore; she was going to get whoever the next person was first. It didn't take long for her to meet her third baby daddy and he was just like the rest.

So at age twenty-one, Mo was expecting another child. The father was a married man who had promised her everything under the sun and again Mo fell for it. He was an educated man, a professor at the community college, and Mo thought she had hit the jackpot even when she came to learn that he was a recreational drug user and a womanizer. At first, he used to take her and Jaheem on weekend getaways and treated her like she was the apple of his eye. He was the first man to buy her a real designer purse; she had the receipt to prove it. But soon after that, Mo found a letter in his jacket pocket when she was looking for some change for the launderette. It was addressed to Mr. and Mrs. Johnson. She shook the envelope in his face.

"What's this?" she started cursing him out "Who's 'Mrs. Johnson'?"

He went into a rage. "Yes, I'm married!" he shouted. "So what? Why'd you want to go and spoil a good thing? And if you think I'll ever leave her for you, you're wrong! She is my retirement package and I am not going to mess that up!" He left the house shouting.

Mo had plenty of stories to tell to gain sympathy. Shavon had heard it all: from the story of Mo losing her wallet with all her money in it at the store and not being able to pay her utility bill so the children were going to be in the dark, to her magnetic strip on her benefit card being demagnetized and she wasn't able to get any cash out of the ATM. It was always puzzling to Shavon how Mo was always broke yet managed to look like she had just finished starring in a music video; she had enough jewelry to start a gold rush in Florida! Mo dressed her daughter Destiny as if she were a fashion plate, and many times Shavon had warned her that dressing a child like a little woman was not a good thing.

"I'm raising her to not be a fool!" was Mo's reply.

"Look," Shavon said, opening her Bible to Proverbs 22:6, "'Train a child in the way he should go, and when he is old he will not turn from it.'"

But Mo just laughed. It was no use, not yet anyway. Shavon knew that she was just going to have to wait for God to deal with Mo in His own way and in His own timing.

The letter on the front door from Mo read: "My girl Shavon, I need a hook-up till the 5th of the month. Tyra needs some pampers and I need to get some gas to go on a job search on Monday. P.S. I need to borrow your silver sandals to wear to the park on next Sunday."

At the bottom she had left three cell phone numbers and an email address. Shavon read the email address and howled with laughter. It was got-2-get it @ yahoo.com.

She thinks she's some business executive, Shavon laughed. All those numbers like she doesn't want to miss out on a contractual deal. Shavon couldn't do anything but love Mo; she was a real character.

After reading the note, Shavon took off her clothes and sat down to eat. Like a starving hostage, she gulped down her food, leaving not a single morsel on her plate. As she took the plate to rinse it, she saw the message light blinking on her answering machine. Probably Pastor Dallas calling to apologize for having my car towed, she thought. But there were six messages. Who could be leaving all those messages?

The first was from Alana wanting to know how church service was and if she had 'turned the church out' with her solo. Alana ended the message by trying to sing a stanza of the song, but the machine cut her right off. Shavon was glad because Alana could not sing her way out of a paper bag! The second and third messages were from Mo wanting to know if Shavon had received her note. She started off with, "Sit down, Jaheem, wait one minute. No, you can have it later, not now. Hey, this is Mo'keisha, Shavon girl, give me a call. Bye." After that was just a lot of yelling. The fourth message was from Kenneth, Shavon's old boyfriend. She wondered why he was calling her; she had cut him off over two years ago because he had the Didn't Disease – he didn't like to work, didn't like to clean up behind himself, didn't like to tell the truth, didn't like to contribute financially to the household, didn't like to act his age, didn't like to be in a monogamous relationship, and surely didn't like to come home.

Shavon knew that living with a man without being married was forbidden according to her faith. She knew that she had compromised her faith when she shacked with Kenneth. Shavon's parents were very disheartened, and on every occasion brought it to her attention. Shavon knew that the next man that she dated, she was going to have to be married, if they were to live together.

What Kenneth was calling about was to see if she was available for dinner later in the evening. She deleted the message in a hurry. He had his way of trying to sway her with his crying and asking for forgiveness while professing that he was a changed man, but she didn't want to be tempted.

The fifth message was from Sister Karen wanting to know if she was going to come to choir rehearsal on Wednesday night and wanting to know why she left before service was over. The sixth was just a hang up.

At long last, time for a nap; but before she lay down on the couch, she looked over at her computer. The screen said there was a current message.

"Mr. Black Emperor," she said. Sure enough, it was from him. As she read the message she almost blushed: "I had a great time chatting with you last night," he wrote. "Sorry for keeping you up so late. I hope I didn't disturb your beauty rest, Beautiful!"

Immediately she responded with, "I was okay. I just woke up a little late. And now I am tired and need a nap. I'm so sleepy that my eyes are closing."

"Go and sleep," came his instant answer.

"Wait," she wrote, "I have a few more questions from last night. What do you do in your spare time?" Of course, what she really wanted to know was if he had time for her, also if he worked.

"I usually hang out with friends or participate in church activities when time permits."

"What do you do for work?" she asked almost shyly.

"I am in the field of financial management." The answer was really broad for Shavon, but at least he had a respectable profession.

Mr. Black Emperor wrote, "So, Beautiful, what do you do for fun when you are not getting your beauty rest?"

She wanted to answer the question intelligently, so she answered "In my spare time, I volunteer once a month at the homeless shelter, sing in my church choir, and occasionally hang out with my best friend Alana for dinner or a movie. Sometimes, I go home and spend time with my parents and brother."

"Are you a city girl or a country girl?" he asked.

Shavon wasn't sure how to answer that. "I was born and raised in Miami – South Beach. I moved to Gator Nation to attend the university."

"Oh, so are you are a Florida girl during football season and a Miami Hurricane when you go home?" he replied.

"I am a die hard Miami Hurricane who lives in Gator Nation." Shavon was fighting to keep her eyelids from closing and looking at the computer screen wasn't helping at all. Reluctantly she wrote, "I'm going to have to call it a day. Sorry, but I will chat with you later today. Okay?"

Back came his reply. "If you need any help getting to sleep let me know!"

Again she almost blushed. "Thanks, but no thanks."

"Sweet dreams," he replied

From a deep sleep, Shavon heard a light tapping on her front window. Was it a dream? Slowly she got up from the couch to look: there were Mo and her Three Musketeers looking hot and sticky. Shavon opened up the door and they all came in sucking up the cool air that awaited them on the inside. Mo looked anxious but started out with small talk as she wiped her brow.

After a few minutes Shavon cut to the chase. "So, Mo, what's up?"

"Well, I been riding around town all day waiting for you to call me back, and I'm exhausted from sitting in that hot car."

"Here, let me get you something cold to drink," said Shavon. "You all look parched." She went to the kitchen, filled a pitcher with apple juice and ice, got some milk for Tyra, and then returned.

"So, Mo, how much money do you need?" she asked as she poured their drinks.

For a moment Mo looked almost like a child. "About a hundred dollars? I got to take care of a few odds and ends."

"Can I write you a check?" Shavon replied.

"No, Vonny girl, I need some cash! A check won't do me any good this time of day and a Sunday, too? No, baby, I need green stuff. Checks are too much of a hassle."

Shavon nodded and got her purse. Remembering that she had quite a lot of cash in her wallet, she quickly pulled out five crispy twenty dollar bills and handed them over. Mo looked like a ton of bricks had just been lifted off of her shoulders. To Shavon, something wasn't right, but she wasn't in the mood to try and pry whatever was going on out of Mo. Instead she'd call her later in the week to see what was up and why she was acting so jittery. Shavon gathered up some fresh fruit and healthy snacks from the kitchen and placed them in a plastic bag for the kids.

"Say thank you," Mo told her kids as she rushed them out the door. "Bye, Vonny. Thanks." She waved and was gone, her hundred dollars tucked neatly in her pocket.

It wasn't ten seconds later when Shavon had just gone to her bedroom when she heard the doorbell ring. To her surprise, it was Jaheem, looking at Shavon like she knew why he was there.

"You left something, sweetie?" she asked.

Jaheem looked in the direction of the car where his mother, Tyra, and Destiny were waiting. "Ms. Vonny, my mama says can she borrow those silver sandals?"

She'd had it. Mo didn't know when enough is enough. "Baby, go back to your mother's car, buckle up and buckle your sisters up, too, and tell your mother I said 'No!' Tell her that I've had one heck of a day and I need to rest. Okay?" She winked at him and closed the door.

She returned to the bathroom to run a bath and set it on jet spa mode. As she watched the steam rise from the tub, she knew her body was in for a treat. Shavon measured out an equal portion of honey-and-milk bath crystals and tossed it into the water. The fragrance immediately filled the room. She popped in her Floetry CD and lit a scented candle. The mood was set. She eased her way into the tub, content, finally able to relax and put the day behind her. She remembered the verse in Philippians 3:13: "Brothers, I do not consider myself yet to have taken hold of it. But one thing I do: Forgetting what is behind and straining toward what is ahead."

While relaxing in the tub, her mind started to drift to Mr. Black Emperor. What was he doing? Was he thinking about her? She leaned back into the steamy water, saying to herself: "Girl, you're thinking about a man you don't even know. You know what, Shavon, you got it bad. You have to stop this. And you are going to have to pray – pray real hard!"

*I waited patiently for the LORD;
and he inclined unto me,
and heard my cry. Psalm 40:1*

Am I in for another heck of a day? Shavon wondered as she cancelled the lunch reservation and rummaged around in her desk drawers for something to eat. It was really too bad, she'd been so looking forward to lunch with her friend.

CHAPTER III

THE NERVE OF SOME PEOPLE

The next morning had come too soon. Shavon felt exceptionally refreshed after over eight hours of sleep. She stretched, feeling like a newborn baby. Today was Monday, it was off to another week. Usually she didn't have to be in the office until 9 a.m. so she decided to check her emails and trash any junk mail that she had received in the last week or so. As she plundered through her email she was stunned to see an email from her father. She didn't know that he knew how to use a computer well enough to send an email.

I've been ignoring my MySpace account, she realized. Shavon had been spending her time chatting with Mr. Black Emperor. She pulled her work planner out of her briefcase to see if she had any early morning appointments. She didn't think she had any pressing events, but felt there was something that she was overlooking. Oh yes, she and Alana had planned a lunch date. She knew she would have to call Alana to remind her. Alana was the queen of forgetting, she always needed a reminder call.

She was about to turn off the computer when she noticed that she had three messages waiting to be read. All three of them were from Mr. Black Emperor. She was tempted, but knew if she started chatting with him now she'd probably be late for work. She decided instead to get dressed while listening to gospel music on the radio. It usually took her way too much time deciding what to wear, and sometimes she wished that she was like her mother who got all her clothes for the week ready on Sunday nights.

After looking through her closet for about five minutes, she decided on a burnt orange sundress that she had bought from Stein Mart. This was one of her favorite stores and she tried to go at least twice a week to browse, invariably finding lovely things for herself or her parents. One day she knew that she would have to shop for her husband and children; how she looked forward to that. She selected some sandals that she had bought last summer from The County Cobbler; they went well with the dress. Gold hoop earrings from her jewelry box were next, then a dab or two of her Chanel cologne.

"The princess of our palace," her father used to call her. Even her two older brothers usually got her whatever she wanted. Shavon knew she was spoiled.

Shavon's mother was a retired teacher in Dade County. Highly respected by her colleagues, she had been nominated for Teacher of the Year two times. Her father was an accountant who had decided to retire at the same time as her mother so they could spend more time together and travel. After thirty-eight years of marriage, they were still in love and looked forward to the time they would have grandchildren to enjoy.

"We get a bit tired of carrying around pictures of our grand-dogs, Fifi and Pebbles," they would say laughing. In fact, they did have a granddaughter, Clayson's daughter Emerald, but they never saw her. Clayson, Shavon's second brother, was thirty-one and addicted to prescription pain pills. He had played college football and was a prominent professional player until an injury occurred. Gradually the pain killers became his God until he lost everything, including his will to live. He lost his house, all his cars, and the lavish lifestyle he had grown accustomed to. The two things he missed most was his fiancée Jasmine and their daughter Emerald. Clayson loved Jasmine with every ounce of his soul; but when he had fallen into a deep spiritual and psychological coma, she packed all of her and Emerald's things and moved away with no forwarding address or any explanation.

Shavon remembered her mother and father having to go to Pittsburgh and physically move Clayton back to Miami where he remained withdrawn and closed down. Shavon had tried many times to get him to come to Gainesville and run football camps for the community. It broke her heart to see her brother so hurt but she knew that God had him in the palm of His hand and all she had to do was just wait and let God have His way in his life.

Shavon's oldest brother, Tarik, was thirty-six and a high school principal in Riverdale, Georgia. He was married to Tiffany who acted like she'd married Donald Trump and therefore expected to be treated like royalty. Tarik and Tiffany had no kids, just their two Yorkies, Fifi and Pebbles. Tarik rose from assistant principal to principal, and Tiffany then got her four-bedroom house, customized Lexus, and the luxury to stay at home and not have to work.

Shavon grabbed her Louis Vuitton briefcase, her purse and keys, and was off to start her day. While waiting for her car to cool off from sitting in the hot garage, she took a moment to pray: Father, sorry for hurrying through the day. I want to thank you for watching over me as I rested peacefully last night. Lord, I ask that you send traveling angels before me as I get on the road to go to work. And please bless all my staff. I pray that their hearts and minds be on one accord this morning. Lord, look after my parents, brothers, friends, and my new friend Mr. Black Emperor, wherever he may be. Lord, I ask all these things in Jesus' name. Father, I love you. Amen.

Just as she was about to leave, she heard the phone ring from the kitchen. She knew exactly who it was – it had to be her mother who called every Monday morning like clockwork. But Shavon decided to let the answering machine answer the call; she would call her voicemail when she was on the road to see if it was actually her. After checking, it was indeed her mother: "Good morning, Sweetheart!" she said in her soft voice. "This is your mother. I hope that you had a good weekend. I was calling to tell you about our single ministry banquet at the church. Call me back and oh, by the way, Sister Green's son, Jarrod, will be home that weekend and she was going to bring him. You remember Jarrod? He just graduated from Harvard Law School. And, Shavon, your daddy is going to have a screening for prostate cancer this Friday. Pray for him. I love you, bye."

The information about her father made Shavon nervous. She remembered what her uncle had gone through. She fumbled to press the number four on her speed dial. She needed to talk with her mother. On the third ring, Shavon's mother picked up. "Shavon baby, how are things going in good ole Gainesville?"

"All is well, Mama," Shavon replied.

"Did you get my message about Jarrod?"

Shavon rolled her eyes. "Mama, stop trying to play cupid." Jarrod...was he the one who wore the really thick glasses? she wondered.

"Mama, is he still wearing those two-inch thick glasses?"

"Shavon Josephine Washington!" her mother exclaimed. "You are not judging that young man by his glasses, are you?"

"Sorry, Mama. But is that him?"

"Yes, it is. He still wears glasses and they are going to help him pass the Florida bar exam!"

Shavon was speechless; her mother did have a point there. "Okay, Mama. Point made. I'll look at my schedule and see what I have planned." She had been so consumed with work that she hadn't been to Miami in months. "And where's the best looking daddy in the whole wide world?" she asked her mother.

"He's gone to the deli on the corner like he has been doing for the last seven years for his apple strudel, black coffee, and newspaper. If I didn't know any better, I would swear he had another woman at that deli! It's the same routine every morning: he wakes up and shaves, bathes and gargles, then makes his morning stroll to Dave's Deli."

Shavon and her mother were still talking as she pulled into the parking lot at work. "Mama, I'm going to have to talk with you later; I'm at work now. I'll call you Thursday night. Tell Clayson I said hi and to stop changing his cell phone number. I tried to call him last week, but the number had been changed again."

"Oh, you know how Clayson is; he can change like the wind," Shavon's mother said with worry in her voice. "Bye, Baby."

Shavon looked in her rearview mirror and saw that she had talked all her lip gloss off, so she refreshed it before waltzing gracefully into the building. The non-profit organization where she worked provided mentoring services to at-risk youth. Shavon's job was to oversee the day-to-day operations, manage the entire budget, and keep the board of directors and her staff of eight satisfied. She had been promoted to this position when she was working as the administrative assistant shortly after graduating from college. During that time, she had learned every aspect of the organization from how to make the best coffee in the office to soliciting for cash match donations. She intended to use every skill she had to move up the corporate ladder. The one thing she hadn't learned in school was to treat others the way she wanted to be treated – she had learned that from her parents. She always made sure to make her rounds from the basement with the housekeeping crew to the fourth floor with the CEO, asking each of them how they were and wishing them a good day.

When Ms. Spann, the former program director and Shavon's predecessor, informed the board that she was retiring after twenty-seven years with the organization, they were relieved. Ms. Spann had some really astounding accomplishments, but the board was looking for fresh ideas. Although Ms. Spann knew the organization inside and out and could crunch the budget right down to the last tenth of a cent, she wasn't one to embrace change.

Known as the Guru of Non-Profit, she was well aware of the legalities of non-profits better than a business attorney. In fact, she would frequently challenge Mr. Davidson, the attorney on the board. She would pull her law books from her shelf and search for statutes until she found what she needed to prove her point. Having graduated with honors and an MBA from Florida State, she knew her information well. When Shavon interviewed for the administrative assistant position, Ms. Spann told her that she really wanted to hire her, but there was one thing that she just couldn't overlook. "What's that?" Shavon asked, alarmed.

"Honey, you graduated from the wrong school!" Ms. Spann said and then laughed hysterically. When she finally stopped laughing, she said, "I expect professionalism at all times." This woman was the real deal without a doubt.

While in the elevator on the way to her office, Shavon thought about Mr. Black Emperor: Why didn't I look at his messages? Especially since I told him I'd chat with him last night. I need to apologize ASAP.

Maria, Shavon's administrative assistant, was not at her desk; but then again, Maria was rarely at her desk. She was rather like the office 'good fairy', always somewhere making sure everyone was okay. Maria was a very hard worker, a devoted mother and wife who took her job very seriously. Although she had some challenges, she had worked hard to get to where she was.

As a teen mother and wife, she had worked her way through community college to get an associates degree in business and office management.

Shortly after taking the director position, Shavon was visiting the janitorial room where Maria then worked, and she was impressed with Maria. She had determination and spunk. She often told Shavon about her desire to work upstairs and use the skills that she had learned while in college. Shavon decided to give her a chance and hired her to be the administrative assistant. She didn't regret it: Maria was trustworthy, efficient, and very dependable. Shavon would never forget the Friday when Maria received her first 'upstairs' paycheck. So overcome when she saw the amount on the check, Maria nearly had a panic attack!

"Oh my God! Oh my God!" she kept repeating. "Oh my God! Someone has made a mistake – look!" She held the check out for Shavon to read.

"Calm down. Take a deep breath," Shavon said looking at the check. It looked fine to her, there weren't any extra zeros. One thousand twelve dollars and three cents. "But that's correct, Maria," she said. "That's not a mistake."

"What?" Maria started to weep. "I've never even held a check in my hands over five hundred dollars in my whole entire life!"

"Well, get used to it." Shavon smiled.

"I've gone from two hundred and ninety-three dollars a month from public assistance to nearly five hundred dollars biweekly to this." Maria wiped her tears away. "Thank you, thank you!"

"Don't thank me," Shavon replied, "thank God! He is the reason for this increase."

As Shavon turned the corner, Maria came out of the bathroom singing a song in Spanish. When she saw Shavon she said, "Good morning, Boss. How was your weekend?"

They chatted for a minute, then Shavon went into her executive suite. After Ms. Spann retired, Shavon redecorated the office to reflect her personality. She hired Wonders by Wanda, a local interior decorator, to give her office a complete makeover from the drab wallpaper and old shag carpet décor to a bold and cheerful African theme that felt like the motherland. Shavon loved it. She pulled her day planner out of her briefcase and called Maria.

"Yes, most worthy boss in the world," said Maria as she entered. "And how can I assist you?"

Shavon grinned; she enjoyed Maria's joking around. "Anything pressing for me today?" she asked.

"Lunch with Alana at one, and I have the travel expense reports from Friday that you need to review and sign, as well as the budget reports for this month" Maria replied.

Shavon tried to think of a nice place she could make a reservation for lunch.

Alana enjoyed eating gourmet food, so Shavon thought about going to a new family-operated restaurant that had just opened called Especially For You. It amazed Shavon that Alana wasn't as big as a double-wide trailer! She could eat enough for two grown men yet never gain a pound. Especially For You had received astounding reviews since they opened. By the grace of God, they had an opening for one o'clock; and after making the reservation, Shavon called Alana who worked for a major retail store as a clothing merchandiser. She had worked for this company while she was in college to earn extra money for her shopping and eating addiction. When she got the job, it was a dream come true. She was the only person Shavon knew who could spend eight to twelve hours on Saturdays shopping and eating. Shavon didn't go with her often because it was like having a part-time job going in and out of every store and hearing the endless merits and downsides of every fashion trend. In restaurants, Alana was the only person Shavon knew who could convince the chef to let her sample several dishes for free: "To give you a review," she would say, thus making them obliged to let her taste whatever she wanted. Most restaurant owners knew her by name.

Shavon didn't like calling Alana at work as the associates who answered the phones were always so rude and unprofessional. Shavon had expressed this to Alana on more than one occasion.

"I don't understand how a major retail store allows its associates to have such poor customer service!" she said.

This occasion was no different:. "Hello, Oh My Goodness". This is Joyce and how may I direct your call?" This greeting sounded like one long word.

"Good morning, Joyce. Is it possible to speak with Alana Saint Clair please?"

The associate paused for a minute and it sounded like she smacked her lips. "Sweetie, she is on the floor. Would you like to leave a message?" The words were polite, the tone was sarcastic.

"No, 'Sweetie'. I'll call her on her cell phone. Have a blessed day and by the way, which aisle is your Midol located on?"

"Excuse me?" she snarled.

"Midol" Shavon repeated.

"On aisle number six in the pharmacy," said Joyce sourly.

"Then, Joyce, I suggest you take a fifteen-minute break and get you some." Shavon didn't like being ugly, but she didn't like being tried either. She knew if the owner and founder of this renowned chain knew how customer service was being delivered, he would turn over in his grave.

She dialed Alana's cell, not expecting her to answer. She didn't know why Alana even had a cell phone since she rarely had it on; and when it was on, she usually didn't know where it was.

One time, Alana lost her phone in a display of women's under-garments and had to back-track her way all around the store, trying to remember where she'd been. She tried calling it but remembered it was on vibrate mode so it wasn't going to ring. She did eventually find it when a customer was looking through the underwear bin and felt something vibrating. The shocked customer took it to customer service and turned it in.

Amazingly Alana answered this time. "What's up? she said. "I left you a message on Sunday. So tell me, did you make the church walls quiver with your solo?"

"I did alright for a city girl," Shavon said, rather proud of herself.

"Girl, I've been working like a slave. I've been trying to order merchandise for our summer explosion sale," said Alana. "I have been working twelve-hour days, six days a week!"

"So are we still on for lunch today?" Shavon asked.

The phone got quiet. Then Alana said, "Vonny, I hate to cancel with you but I've got to get this project done."

Shavon had been really looking forward to having lunch with Alana. Since they had both started their careers, they hardly ever got together anymore, and Alana spent a lot of time with Drayton, her boyfriend.

Drayton and Alana had met when he was a senior in college and she was a sophomore; six years later, they were still together and really happy. Drayton had majored in sports psychology then moved to Davie, Florida to attend Nova Southeastern University so he could pursue his masters in clinical psychology; but he called and emailed Alana regularly while he was away, sending her unexpected cards and gifts.

Am I in for another heck of a day? Shavon wondered as she cancelled the lunch reservation and rummaged around in her desk drawers for something to eat. It was really too bad; she'd been so looking forward to lunch with her friend.

But they that wait upon the LORD shall renew their strength; they shall mount up with wings as eagles; they shall run, and not be weary; and they shall walk, and not faint. Isaiah 40:31

Let integrity and uprightness preserve me; for I wait on thee. Psalm 25:21

Shavon, feeling a little spooked remembering that tale, decided to review Mr. Black Emperor's profile again to see if he could fit the profile of a psychopath. She knew this was hard to detect from a computer screen but she was going to look again. No, it all seemed fine, and like her, he didn't have any pictures in his photo gallery. She wondered if it was time to ask him about it...

CHAPTER IV

OH WHAT A MANIC MONDAY

The traffic on the way home that evening was crazy. Normally it took her about thirty-five minutes to get home, but today it took almost twice as long due to unexpected road construction. Mondays were not Shavon's favorite day, but she had done almost everything that she was supposed to do at work – reviewed all the travel expenses, written the agenda for the next board of directors' meeting, scheduled an appointment with her grant writer to discuss financial opportunities, and even had time to water her plants.

Hot, she wished that she was in Miami near the beach and could race into the cooling water as she had as a child. There were no beaches in Gainesville, and the nearest one that she liked was in Daytona.

When she had bought this house, she was really torn because it didn't have a pool. She was born to be a mermaid; and on a hot day like today, she could really use a good swim.

Shavon pulled halfway into her driveway so she could gather her mail, something she rarely did since she paid all her bills online. There was a large heap of mail, though most of it was junk: catalogs, magazines she didn't subscribe to, credit card applications, and a few letters for her neighbor that were misrouted to her home. She'd take them over to them at a later time.

Inside she followed her usual routine: she kicked her shoes off, tossed her keys and purse on the counter, then browsed through the refrigerator. She hadn't been to the grocery store in about two weeks, so there wasn't much in there. She poured herself a tall glass of cran grape, the same juice her father so enjoyed and from whom she had learned to like it. He claimed that cranberry juice cleanses your kidneys. She was really hungry, having eaten only a pack of stale peanut butter crackers at her desk after being stood up by Alana.

In the freezer was a Lean Cuisine meal; (not something she was wildly fond of, but it would have to do since she didn't feel like going out again; not even to the gym although she knew it was time for a good workout). She was a member of Fitness Forever Club, a hot spot for college students who monopolized the whole gym.

As she heated her 'frozen dinner delight', she thought about the parking lot and towing drama of yesterday and realized that she needed to call the church and make an appointment to speak with Pastor Dallas. What a strange incident it had been: what kind of point was Pastor trying to make by having the car towed yet paying the fee for her? Well whatever his point was, she needed to apologize to him.

After eating, she showered and put on her comfortable pajamas to maybe watch a little television or log on to chat with Mr. Black Emperor. As she was brushing her hair, she caught a glimpse of a picture of her parents on the bureau. That morning, her mother had told her that her father had to have a prostate screening. Although Shavon didn't know what it all consisted of, she knew it could be serious. She sighed; if only she could protect her parents from illness. She didn't know how she would deal with her parents not being in her life, especially her father. Of course she loved her mother deeply, but she'd always been a true daddy's girl. When she was about seven, her friends Kelly and Shawn had asked her who she was going to marry when she grew up.

"My daddy of course!" she'd answered them.

"Don't be silly, you can't marry your daddy," Kelly said.

"Why not?" Shavon wanted to know.

"Because he's already married to your mama!" said Kelly.

"Oh." Shavon hadn't thought about that. "Okay, well I'll find a man just like him, and I'll marry him instead, see? Or maybe I will give that man to my mama and then I can marry daddy."

Shavon smiled as she recalled that. Please God, protect daddy and help him through this screening, she prayed silently.

Now would be a good time to look through her mail, but what she really wanted to do was log on to see if Mr. Black Emperor was online. To her delight, he was; but before she started chatting with him, she needed to check her profile as it had been a few months since she had created her site and she needed to make sure she was presenting herself decently. Even though it was a Christian site, Shavon had seen some profiles that made it apparent that some people didn't realize this because they had posted inappropriate information and photos that were way too raunchy. Shavon hadn't even posted a photo because she wanted anyone who read her profile to be fascinated by her personality, not her looks. Maybe it was arrogant, but she felt fairly confident that she could attract any man with her looks; she was a head turner. That was a fact that was affirmed almost every day.

She wondered if maybe she should edit some of the personal information on her profile. She'd heard of despicable internet predators who sought out women on the net with intentions other than friendship, and she'd read articles where internet relationships had gone bad; she didn't want to be another sad statistic.

She was an intelligent woman, surely she'd know if she was getting suckered into something that wasn't right. Still, it was better to be cautious, even with Mr. Black Emperor. She recalled a tragic story about a lonely woman from New Hampshire who was communicating with a man who professed to be a prominent doctor from China. After a year of chatting with him, she agreed to meet him in Canada for a week so she went there to be with him. Within two days of being there, he brutally raped and killed her in the hotel room they shared. It didn't take long for law enforcement to find him; all they had to do was read her emails which outlined all her plans to meet him and the itinerary. It turned out that he was a convicted rapist from Chicago who should not have been walking around free.

Shavon, feeling a little spooked remembering that tale, decided to review Mr. Black Emperor's profile again to see if he could fit the profile as a psychopath. She knew this was hard to detect from a computer screen but she was going to look again. No, it all seemed fine and, like her, he didn't have any pictures in his photo gallery. She wondered if it was time to ask him about it. But before that, she read the unread emails he had sent her.

She clicked into the first email: "Hi," it said, with a smiley face icon. "Guess you're still sleeping - Have a blessed night, Beautiful. "Sleep Tight."

The second, posted at 11:17 pm, read: "No wonder you're so beautiful, you make sure you get all your beauty rest. Talk with you tomorrow - Mr. Black Emperor. Goodnight."

The third, posted at 9:37am that morning, read: "I thought about you all night long. Email me when you get a chance. I really enjoy our conversations."

The final email, posted at 3:20 that afternoon, said: "You are one busy woman. Talk with you soon. I hope you're okay and I hope you are having a great day."

Shavon read them several times over, feeling bad that she hadn't woken up yesterday to chat with him as she'd promised.

She logged on. "Hello?" she wrote.

His reply came almost instantly. "Hello to you, too! I am glad that you haven't forgotten me. I figured maybe I had talked you to death!"

"First let me apologize for not getting back to you on Sunday," she typed. "I did take a nap but it rolled over into the next morning because I was extremely tired."

"Don't worry, Beautiful. I'm glad you caught up on some sleep. How was your day?"

"It was okay," she replied. "I went to work and came home; that's about it. Nothing to write home about."

"So tell me, Beautiful, what brings you to the world of cyberspace?"

"Basically I was curious about this Christian dating community, so I decided to join and here I am." She went on to explain that she had read about it in a Christian magazine and had figured it couldn't hurt, so she gave it a shot. "And I'm glad I did," she added, feeling bold.

"I'm glad you did, too," said Mr. Black Emperor. "I was on Black Planet for a bit, but I was a little too slow for that crowd!"

Shavon laughed. "Yeah, I heard Black Planet was mostly a bit confusing."

"Well I'm glad that I chose this site instead," he wrote, "because it has warranted me the opportunity to get to know you."

Shavon was pleased he was good with words. "Now tell me, 'Emperor', how come you don't have pictures in your photo gallery?"

"I am not camera friendly, plus why reveal the whole package? If a person is mostly interested in looks, then they wouldn't be worth my time."

"I buy that," she replied. She really wanted to ask him to send her a photo. The image in her mind was that he was tall with smooth coffee-with-creamer skin, hair cut close to his head, broad shoulders and a muscular physique, and straight teeth. She couldn't stand men who didn't have good dental hygiene. Still, rather than ask for a photo, she wrote: "Mr. Black Emperor, what is your birth name?"

"My family calls me Junior, but the name is Travis Elliot."

"Travis! Okay! So Travis, why do they call you Junior?"

Travis seemed to hesitate for a few seconds. "I was named after my father, Travis Elliot Sr., but I never knew him. I was raised by my mother and older sister Belinda in a small town in Mississippi. You probably never heard of Yazoo, Mississippi. I've heard from other family members that my father was a traveling evangelist and must have had a few late night Bible studies with my mama."

Shavon was gratified that he was being so candid, so when he asked her to tell him a bit more about herself, she gladly told him about her family and her childhood.

"You were blessed to have both parents growing up," Travis wrote. "Tell me more, I enjoy it." For some time, Shavon told him more details about her life, growing up in Miami, how happy she had been as a kid, and how her parents still really loved each other. In return, Travis told her that he could only imagine what it was like growing up with both parents. His mother was a domestic housekeeper and they were dirt poor. He grew up wearing hand-me-down clothes, and his mother barely had enough money to send him to a movie downtown. He was raised on rice with chicken neck gravy, and his mother could 'cook or burn', as they said in Mississippi about good cooks. She earned extra money by selling dinners on the weekends.

When Travis was in middle school, he used to deliver dinners to his mother's customers while his friends were enjoying Friday night football games at the local school. By saving the occasional tips, he was able to buy his own shoes. His mother wasn't very educated, but she used the gifts that God had given her to make her way in life and provide for her children. Her constant prayer for her son was that God would give him the opportunity to get out of Yazoo to make a better life for himself.

His sister, Belinda, took care of him all his life while their mother struggled to make a living, so she was more like his mother than their actual mother. "I'll be forever grateful for Belinda's commitment to me," he wrote, "she is a wonderful sister. Now your turn. What brought you to and kept you in Gator Nation?"

Shavon, moved by his story, explained how after she graduated from college, she decided to stay in Gainesville, purchase a home, and make a career there. "I needed to start life for myself away from my parents," she wrote.

"Pretty independent," he wrote. "I like a woman who knows what she wants and goes after it."

Shavon was smiling broadly. It was great getting to know him better, and it was nice to share things with him about her family. Yes, he was right. She was blessed to have such a loving family.

"On a different subject," she wrote "what is your favorite restaurant in town?"

"Well, I love soul food. I like Mama's Place on University Blvd, but I heard that June Bug's Soul Food Shack is even better. You know, he added, obviously in a nostalgic mood, "that reminds me of how Mama sometimes used to make salmon croquets and grits for me on Saturday mornings before she left for work and we would sit at the table. I'd tell her about my school projects and she would just sit there smiling and listening. But, you know, I don't think she really knew what I was talking about; I think she just liked hearing me talk. Hey listen to me, would you; you ask about restaurants and I give you all this about my mother! Sorry!"

"No, I love hearing it all. I really do. And guess what else? June Bug's Soul Food Shack is my absolute favorite, though I heard that Mama's Place is great, too."

"Yes, Beautiful, the food there is to die for. The collard greens with smoked pig tails are mouth-watering good, and the smothered pork chops are great." Travis added that his favorite was the butter pecan pound cake with a scoop of butter pecan ice cream.

Shavon told him how when she first came to Gainesville, she used to go to Mama Lula's restaurant where she could get a piece of fried chicken, yellow rice, and cabbage with cornbread for less than four dollars. "But food prices have sky-rocketed, just like the price of gas. So, who's your favorite college team?"

"I love the Miami Hurricanes, but now the Gators are growing on me," he replied.

"You're just saying that because I'm from Miami!" she wrote, teasing him. "Do you remember any exceptional players from the late nineties?"

Travis wrote that Miami had a good team back them, but there was one player who was spectacular. "His name was Clayson, Clayson Washington. He was the most recruited quarterback in the nation and was drafted by the Pittsburgh Steelers where he played a few years before he had a major injury that ended his football career. The last thing I heard about him was that he was somewhere in Miami homeless and had suffered a nervous breakdown. It makes me mad how the NFL doesn't do well in rehabilitating their players after such a tragic loss like his. Clayson made the Steelers a lot of money, yet they didn't do much at all to help him when he needed help."

"You're right, but Clayson is not homeless. He lives in the guesthouse on his parents' property" said Shavon matter-of-factly.

"How do you know all that?" Travis asked.

"He's my brother!" she answered.

"Your brother? Clayson Washington? No! That's incredible!"

"He breaks my heart" Shavon said sadly. "He's so depressed and aimless. He really was amazing in his playing days. I get choked up when I think about him. He's such a good person, he loves people, he loves football, and now he walks around lifeless." She told Travis about Clayson's daughter Emerald whom he hadn't seen in what seemed like a decade.

"I can hardly believe what I am hearing!" exclaimed Travis. "Clayson Washington's sister. Clayson is the superhero of football in my eyes."

"Sometimes I can't understand how God can allow him to endure so much pain." Shavon looked over at the clock above her computer. They'd been chatting for several hours. It was time for her to get some sleep if she didn't want to wake up late again. "Emperor – Travis, I'm sorry. I love chatting with you, but I am going to have to say goodnight. I'm so tired."

"Yes, me too" he agreed. "I loved chatting with you again, especially since we now know more about each other. Sleep well, Beautiful. Have a peaceful night."

Reluctantly Shavon said goodnight, logged off and prepared for bed. Ever since she was a little girl, she had always said her prayers before going to bed and tonight was no different. She knelt beside her bed and said a prayer for Clayson in his recovery, then for her daddy, and for her mother to have the strength to endure all the trials she was facing. She prayed for her staff, for Alana and Drayton, and now for her Mr. Black Emperor.

She was fast asleep when the phone rang. Startled, she looked at the digital clock on her dresser; it was 2:30 am. In a fog, she saw the caller ID: Department of Corrections. She turned on the light, and her heart started pounding as she answered the phone.

My soul, wait thou only upon God; for my expectation is from him. Psalm 62:5

I am weary of my crying: my throat is dried: mine eyes fail while I wait for my God. Psalm 69:3

With her heart beating wildly, she hung up. There was no way she could call her parents at this hour; it would give them both heart attacks. She felt as if a ton of bricks had been dumped on her head. "Lord," she prayed with her head bowed, "I am so confused right now. I don't know what is going on; but Lord, please give me the strength to endure this situation."

CHAPTER V

CLOSURE FOR CLAYSON

Shavon thought she was having some type of crazy dream. The person on the other end of the line asked for Shavon Washington.

"This is Shavon Washington," she replied, thinking: oh God, please let nothing have happened to Clayson or my parents. The last time that Clayson had gone out on the town, he had too many beers and was stopped by the police. Instead of giving them her parents' number, he had given them her number.

The man on the line introduced himself as Detective Andrew Smith and explained that he was calling from the Washington, DC police department. He had been given her number by Ms. Jasmine Richardson and was calling in reference to Emerald Trinity Washington, Ms. Richardson's minor child.

Shavon was confused; why would the police be calling her about Jasmine and Emerald? What was going on?

"Ms. Washington, we have Ms. Jasmine Richardson in custody for attempted murder and we need someone to care for her daughter. She says the child is your biological niece."

"Attempted murder?" asked Shavon in astonishment. This was surreal.

"That's right ma'am," said Detective Smith. He asked when she could get there and told her that until a family member could get there, Emerald would be placed in temporary foster care with the State under the Child Protection Law.

Shavon pulled herself together. "I'll be there tomorrow by 5 pm at the latest." With trembling fingers she wrote down the address on the back of a book on her nightstand.

With her heart beating wildly, she hung up. There was no way she could call her parents at this hour; it would give them both heart attacks. She felt as if a ton of bricks had been dumped on her head. "Lord," she prayed with her head bowed, "I am so confused right now. I don't know what is going on; but Lord, please give me the strength to endure this situation."

She thought about the conversation with Detective Smith. It sounded really serious.

Jasmine, who Shavon had always thought of as a very loving mother to Emerald, had been charged with attempted murder. How could that be possible? Jasmine had a stand-offish persona about her, but she certainly didn't seem capable of murder! Since dropping off the face of the earth when Clayson went through his dilemma, her parents had been sending Jasmine monthly child support payments for Emerald via a post office box in South Carolina. The payments came from Clayson's last four years of NFL pension.

Shavon got out of bed; she had to get organized. She called her office and left a message for Maria, informing her that she had a family emergency so she wouldn't be in for the rest of the week. "I'll try and come in early, around 7:00, to explain some details," she said. "But if I don't make it in, I'll call later in the day."

She threw enough under garments and outfits into her Louis Vuttion duffle bag for at least one week, not caring which clothes her hands alighted on, just wanting the necessities. Then she logged onto South West Airlines to reserve a one-way ticket to Washington, DC that morning. She booked the reservation, figuring she could drive a rental car back. Then she booked a room at a Marriot near the police headquarters and arranged for a rental car so she could get around town. She hadn't seen Emerald in years; but this was her niece; she needed to get there to help.

She really wasn't sure if she was up to the full responsibility of bringing Emerald home with her, since she hadn't really had much experience with children besides one weekend when Mo had asked her to watch the children for a few minutes, which turned out to be a whole wild weekend!

Shavon set her alarm for 6:00 am to try and get a couple of hours of sleep before facing what would surely be a difficult day. She would need to call her parents to tell them what was going on; Emerald was their only grandchild and she knew they would want her protected. Her parents could tell Clayson, she decided; there was no way she wanted to handle that. She knew it would either take him over the edge or save his life.

Miraculously, she managed to sleep until her alarm went off at 6:00. Had she dreamt it all? No, there it was on her caller ID: Department of Corrections. At 7:00, she dialed her parent's number, the same number they had since she was in grade school. She hoped her father would pick up and that he had not left for the deli yet. Their phone number was only one digit off from Blockbuster's number, so her parents frequently got calls inquiring about movies. Shavon's dad would say, "Sure, why not! Let me get your name and number, then I will call Blockbuster and see if they have it in." Shavon's mother had called the store numerous times to inform them but nothing ever happened.

The phone rang twice before her mother answered.

Her mouth dry, her stomach in knots, Shavon spoke: "Good morning, Mommy."

"What's wrong?" her mother said immediately. "Why are you calling me 'Mommy'? What's happened?" She was right, the only time Shavon called her Mommy was when something was wrong.

Shavon could hardly speak.

"Shavon Washington, what is wrong? Has Kenneth been harassing you again?"

"No, Mommy. It's about…"

"He'd better not be annoying you again. We had enough problems with all that."

"Please, Mommy. Listen to me! It's about Emerald and Jasmine. Seems like..."

"She badgering you for money?"

Shavon took a deep breath. "Listen to me, please! You need to let me explain without interrupting." She told her mother about the late-night phone call, the conversation with the detective, and how Emerald was being placed in temporary foster care. Ignoring her mother's frightened interjections, she told her that she was flying there today to get Emerald and bring her to Florida. Then she heard the phone drop and her mother weeping loudly.

"Please get back on!" Shavon called loudly, a few times. "Please! Pick up the phone, Mommy."

"Shavon, your father and I must come and meet you there," said her mother after pulling herself together. "Give me the flight details and I'll call you back in thirty minutes."

"Call me on my cell," Shavon said after giving her the flight information. "I need to get into the office for a bit."

As she put her bags in the car, Shavon wished she could call Travis to talk to him about all this. To think that just last night they'd been talking about Clayson – how bizarre! But one person she would have to call was Sister Karen, or maybe Maria could call her to explain there was some unexpected family business so she would not be at choir rehearsal that week.

She called Alana at home and told her what was happening. Alana asked if there was anything that she could do. "You know I love your family," she said. "I've often prayed for the reunion of Emerald and Clayson. I'm just sorry it had to happen this way."

At the office, Maria handed her a pastry, some fresh fruit and a caramel latte on a small silver tray. "I figured you wouldn't have eaten," she said, "and you need something in your stomach with all this going on."

Maria had already printed out the board's agenda for the meeting next week so Shavon could critique it and had also charged up the office laptop computer for Shavon to take with her.

"You're great, Maria," Shavon said, eating her breakfast gratefully. "Thank you."

"Your mother's on line two," Maria buzzed a moment later.

Shavon picked up the phone. "Mommy, before you speak, I want you to know that everything will be alright."

"Thanks, Baby," her mother replied, then told her they'd made all the necessary arrangements and would meet her at the police headquarters at 5:00 that afternoon, "We love you, Baby, be strong and we'll see you later today."

Shavon was curious if her parents had told Clayson or not, but now wasn't a good time to ask. She dialed the number for the DC police station and asked for Detective Smith.

"Detective Smith speaking. How I may help you?" he said as soon as the call went through.

Shavon told him she was calling regarding Jasmine Richardson and her daughter Emerald Trinity Washington and that both she and her parents were arriving in DC that afternoon and would like to meet with him. He agreed to meet them all at 5:00.

With just over an hour to catch her flight, Shavon gathered up the laptop and thanked Maria again. Maria hugged her. "Call me when you get there. Have a good flight," she said as she waved goodbye to Shavon.

As she drove to the airport, it dawned on Shavon that she should call her brother Tarik. He certainly deserved to know what was going on. She called his home number and got the answering machine. "You have reached the Washington residence," said Tiffany's prissy voice. "Please leave a message immediately following the beep. For Tarik press one, for Tiffany press two, for Fifi and Pebbles press three."

Shavon sighed. Tiffany had really lost her mind. She hung up, deciding to call Tarik at work. A woman with a Jamaican accent answered. "Martin Luther King Jr. High School. Alda speaking. How can I assist you?"

Shavon asked to speak with Mr. Washington. "This is Shavon Washington," she stated.

"Please hold," the woman said with deep cynicism in her voice. She must have not hit the hold button because Shavon could hear everything she was saying. "Mr. Washington's wife is calling, disguising her voice again. It must be fantasy week for the Washingtons." Shavon heard women giggling. Tiffany probably really worked Tarik's staff's nerves .

"Hello, Tarik Washington speaking," her brother said.

"Hello, Mr. Washington, this is your baby sister."

"Vonny! What a nice surprise. How are you doing?" Tarik said, sounding delighted.

Slowly Shavon told him what was happening. "Right now we don't know anything other than that, but I'll call you as soon as we know more, okay?"

"Of course – this is terrible!" he replied. "What can I do to help? How is Clayson handling it?"

She told him that Mama hadn't mentioned anything about that, so she didn't know. "Tarik, just one other thing," she added. "Why do Fifi and Pebbles have a voicemail box?"

He laughed. "That's a million dollar question, Vonny. To tell you the truth, I only pay the phone bill and that's about it. I don't ask any questions."

As Shavon boarded the plane, she saw that she would be sitting next to a Beyonce Knowles impersonator. The girl had the look all the way down to the bulky hair weave. She even had the Sasha Fierce attitude. Shavon slid into her window seat while giving her a smile; but the girl, irritated that Shavon had to get past her, rolled her eyes so hard that when Shavon glanced back to look at her, her eyes seemed crossed. Shavon didn't want to make small talk nor did she need hostility; she wanted to be quiet and try to enjoy the flight.

CHAPTER VI

ON THE WAY TO DC

As Shavon boarded the plane, she saw that she would be sitting next to a Beyonce Knowles impersonator. The girl had the look all the way down to the bulky hair weave. She even had the Sasha Fierce attitude. Shavon slid into her window seat while giving her a smile; but the girl, irritated that Shavon had to get past her, rolled her eyes so hard that when Shavon glanced back to look at her, her eyes seemed crossed. Shavon didn't want to make small talk nor did she need hostility; she wanted to be quiet and try to enjoy the flight. She gave the girl a look that said 'don't try me', then pulled out her laptop to check her email. Two were from Travis. She smiled. The first included an attachment which she opened. It was a clip from Kirk Franklin's video "Looking for You".

How sweet, she thought. She would email him regarding her whereabouts and tell him what was going on; she was starting to feel like she could be open with him about anything. The second email from Travis was equally as pleasing: "Beautiful, I confess that I had a good time talking with you. I confess I would love to talk to you again. And the highlight of my confession is that I miss you."

Below the letter was a button that said "click here." Once clicked, Usher's "Confessions" song blared from the speakers. Shavon's seatmate started bobbing her head wildly while swaying to the beat. "That's my song right there. Hey, hey!" she said bouncing about in her seat. A few other passengers also turned to look at Shavon. Oh Lord, they must think I'm a hood rat, Shavon thought, fumbling to turn off the sound.

"Sorry," she said, looking about her. But inside she was happy. Travis' gesture made her feel special. He was winning her over and it felt wonderful. Just calling him Travis instead of Mr. Black Emperor felt good.

When the plane was preparing to land, Shavon muttered, "Thank you, Lord. Thank you for a good flight and thank you for working out this situation." According to Romans 4:17, Shavon was speaking those things as though they were.

Just as she was leaving the baggage claim area she heard someone call, "Hey, you!"

Shavon turned and saw the Beyonce look-alike shoving a business card at her. "If you ever want your nails fly like these," she extended her hand to show them off, "call or email me for an appointment."

Grinning, Shavon took the card. "Okay, thanks." She pocketed the card and walked down the corridor to the rental car department. While waiting for the Hertz representative to process everything, she pulled the card out of her pocket and read it: Naughty Girls Nail Salon. Owner/Operator: Kee Kee Brown. Mon-Thurs 10 am-10 pm. The email address startled Shavon: uaintready4this@hotmail.com. She shook her head. "I bet that shop is one hot mess," she said to herself.

After only a few wrong turns and almost being run off the road a couple of times, Shavon arrived at the Marriott. She'd driven in Georgia and New York, but all that was nothing compared to driving in D.C. Once in her hotel room, she took a long shower and then ordered a Mexican mixed sampler and raspberry tea from room service. As she was eating, her mother called to tell her they'd arrived and were staying at the Marriott on Lenox Road.

"You're kidding," said Shavon. "So am I!"

"We're going to take a shower and then have a short nap, so let's all meet in the lobby at 4:15," said her mother.

Before getting dressed, Shavon logged on to see if Travis was there. He wasn't, so she sent him an email. "Thank you for your two lovely emails. I have a funny story to tell you about that song from Usher. I listened to it on a flight. It's not such a good idea to listen to music without earphones when you're on a plane!" She told him where she was and why she was there, then finished by telling him she would try and log in that evening to see if he was online. "And," she added, "my name is Shavon. I like being called 'Beautiful', but that's my real name."

At 4:15pm, Shavon scurried downstairs wearing a light grey business pant suit and flat shoes after she had toned down her makeup. She wanted Detective Smith to feel like she and her family were appropriate enough to care for Emerald. As she got off the elevator, she saw her dad wearing a pair of khaki Dockers and a Hawaiian printed shirt. He looked like he had lost a few pounds, but he looked well. Her mother was wearing a conservative peach-colored two-piece suit and had pulled her hair into a modest bun. Shavon ran to them and gave them a group hug. Her father kissed her. "You're so pretty, Baby Girl," he said.

Shavon smiled. She loved knowing that she was still the apple of her daddy's eye. The three of them rode to the police station in silence. Shavon had put the car radio on, but no one was listening.

"How's your job going?" her father said to finally break the silence.

"It's good, Dad. I have a wonderful staff and the pay isn't bad either." She glanced at him, smiling.

"Yes, yes, I am putting something aside for my retirement." She glanced at her mother in the rearview mirror. "Mama, did you get a chance to talk with Clayson?"

Dad jumped in. "We did, yes. And, Baby, you should've seen the look on his face! It was like the old Clayson had returned for a few minutes. He wanted to come too, but we told him we needed to get more details and we'd call him as soon as we found out more."

"He went straight to the guest bedroom in the house and knelt down to pray," interrupted her mother. "He was so overwhelmed that his baby has finally been located, even under these circumstances."

As soon as Shavon parked the car, they walked into the police station and told the female officer at the reception desk that they had an appointment with Detective Smith. She nodded, "Follow me," after handing them all visitors' badges. They accompanied her to a conference room that seemed to lack any definition. There was only one picture on the wall; it was an older black man wearing a police uniform with many medals pinned to it. The plaque below read: Lieutenant Daniel Walker. He Died With Honor. R.I.P.

Shortly after they were seated, a tall man in his late fifties arrived. He looked like an older version of Michael Jordan, especially with his bald head and welcoming smile.

"Detective Smith," he said extending his hand. He smiled a wide easy smile that instantly eased the tension in the room. As he arranged papers from a folder on the table, Detective Smith said he knew it was difficult to meet under these circumstances, but he was confident this matter could be resolved in no time.

Shavon's father started out by talking about Clayson and Jasmine's relationship. He told the detective that when Clayson was discharged from the Pittsburgh Steelers, Jasmine had mysteriously disappeared with Emerald, leaving no forwarding address. "About two years ago, we got a letter from an attorney in South Carolina petitioning for child support," he said. "The order was for nine hundred and fifty-three dollars a month and Clayson didn't want to contest it; so since then, we've sent a monthly money order for one thousand dollars to a post office box that we were directed to by the attorney."

Shavon was looking at her father and could see that he was getting very emotional. Her mother must have seen the same thing as she took over. She told the detective that when Clayson's lawyer tried to contact Ms. Richardson's lawyer about visitation rights, they never heard from them again. Soon after that, Clayson just gave up.

"That's all good information," said Detective Smith. "I'll document it." He went on to speak of what he knew about Jasmine; she had stated she had no real family and had been raised in a second foster home when her first adoptive mother died. Shavon knew that Jasmine had been adopted but she never knew much about the circumstances behind her family situation. She felt sad for Jasmine; it couldn't be easy to go through this ordeal without family.

"Ms. Richardson was adamant about wanting Emerald to be raised with her father," the detective continued. "She signed the paperwork voluntarily, releasing her parental rights to the child into the custodial care of Clayson and his family."

"What are the charges against her?" Shavon's father asked nervously.

Detective Smith explained what he knew; that Jasmine had been dating a known Cuban art smuggler named Hector. The Feds had been tracking them both since 2006. Three weeks ago, Jasmine had left with Emerald and Hector had been trying to find her – he had his mob connection looking for her as well. On that particular night, he found her in a hotel and threatened to kill both her and Emerald.

"From Ms. Richardson's statement," continued the detective, "he'd apparently given her a gun a few years back, and she used that same gun to shoot and kill him. She said it was self-defense, and she was afraid for her life and the life of her daughter. She shot him once in the chest area and he died from that single gun shot wound."

He went on to describe how Emerald was asleep at the time, but awoke to the commotion. Jasmine grabbed Emerald and a few things and fled the scene. A visitor who was staying at the hotel heard the shot, witnessed Jasmine and the child fleeing, and called the police. Less than three hours later, Jasmine was apprehended and arrested without resistance. She was allowed to stay with Emerald in a single holding cell, hugging her child tightly until a representative from the State Child's Protective Services arrived to interview her.

"Ms. Richardson instructed one of our detectives to retrieve a paper bag from the car she was driving," Detective Smith said. "Mr. and Mrs. Washington, I think you need to see this." He handed a small shiny shopping bag to Shavon's father who pulled out a sealed envelope addressed to Clayson and them. Inside were all of Emerald's school, shot, and medical records, as well as her birth certificate and social security card. At the bottom of the bag was a box that contained all of the child support money orders that Shavon's parents had ever sent, completely untouched. It amounted to almost $24,000.

Mr. and Mrs. Washington shook their heads in disbelief while Shavon wondered if Jasmine had prepared herself for this day. It all seemed so neat, so well organized.

"Can we see Emerald?" Shavon's father asked.

"Yes. She's here," replied Detective Smith. "We asked a social worker to bring her in." He turned to Shavon to tell her that Jasmine wanted to speak with her in private. Shavon agreed, of course.

"Right, I'll go and talk with the social worker so we can bring Emerald in," the detective said as he stood and started to leave the room. There was not a dry eye in view. Shavon's father was blotting his eyes with a handkerchief while her mother was sniffling to hold back her tears. At the door, Detective Smith stopped and looked back at Shavon. "Ms. Washington, could you follow me? I'll take you to Ms. Richardson now before I bring the girl in."

Nervously Shavon followed him out of the room. It had been such a long time since she had seen Jasmine, and the time between had been so painful for Clayson. Shavon was led to a small bleak room with a wooden table and two chairs. She sat at the table for about five minutes before the door opened and in walked a woman who resembled Jasmine, but looked many years older.

Jasmine had long silky black hair and was slim, whereas this woman had short brown hair and was at least forty pounds overweight. Shocked, Shavon stared at her; what had happened? She looked as if she'd had life sucked out of her. She rose as Jasmine walked towards her and hugged her tightly, as if she were trying to absorb some life from Shavon's body. Shavon held back a sob. They sat, awkwardly, shyly.

"Shavon, I want to say that I am terribly sorry for the pain I have caused your family," Jasmine said slowly. "I am sincerely sorry."

"No, please. Don't go there," replied Shavon. "I'm here to tell you that we will take good care of Emerald."

Weeping softly, Jasmine thanked her. "Please let her always know that her mother loves her; keep me alive in her life. Please allow her to write me; and when you can, bring her to visit me wherever I am going." She looked away, then back again. "I won't harass your family, I won't reach out to her until you all say it's time. Thank you for being here; I needed you so desperately. I called you the other day, but hung up. I didn't know how you'd react to me after all this time."

Shavon reached across the table and squeezed Jasmine's hand. "We are always here for you and Emerald. Thank you for believing in us and trusting us to raise Emerald." Her heart was breaking for Jasmine; how had she been reduced to such a pitiful woman? How sad that in all this time she hadn't reached out; they would have rushed to help her.

"Jasmine, do you know where your biological mother is?"

Jasmine shook her head. "No. She might be in New Orleans. I don't know. Why?"

"I wondered if it would be a comfort to you to be in contact with her."

Jasmine gave a small sad smile. "I doubt it. Emerald is my family, she's all I have."

Feeling a bit shy, Shavon asked Jasmine if she believed in Jesus Christ.

Jasmine shrugged. "I suppose so. I don't know."

"Will you let me help you?" Shavon asked. "You have nothing to lose and everything to gain by accepting Jesus into your life." She bowed her head and reached out for Jasmine's hands. "Father, your daughter Jasmine comes before you today, acknowledging you as her savior. She wants to be saved. You said in your word that all one had to do is confess and she has done that. Let her believe with her heart that you are God, and you died for her sins. Lord, I ask that you bring closure for Jasmine today; I pray that you strengthen her where she is torn down, I ask that you look beyond her faults and see her needs. Lord, she is troubled and needs your comfort. Lord, give her assurance that everything will be alright. Lord, show her your love. Amen."

Just as Shavon was raising her head, the guard entered. It was time to leave.

"Thank you, Shavon," said Jasmine. "You're a good woman. I am blessed that my daughter will be with you and your family." Standing she said, "And would you please tell Clayson that my love is like a river, forever flowing in his direction."

"I will," Shavon replied nodding.

"Really. I am sincere in that," Jasmine added.

"Yes, I know. I can feel it. Goodbye for now, Jasmine. Be strong and know that Emerald will be deeply loved and cared for."

Jasmine was escorted out while Shavon was allowed to sit and weep for a while before she was taken back to the conference room to join her parents there.

Her mother rose to hug her. "Baby," she said, wiping away the tears that had fallen down Shavon's face. "How is she?"

"She'll be alright," Shavon said. "She needs our prayers and our love."

Detective Smith put his head round the door. "You folks ready to meet an angel?"

They all stood as the door opened and in came Emerald. Indeed she was an angel – she was absolutely beautiful! She had long, flowing, silky black hair like Jasmine used to have, and astoundingly clear hazel brown eyes. Her skin was flawless, and she seemed taller than the average seven-year-old. But what struck them all was how much she looked like Clayson.

Detective Smith, holding her hand, started to introduce her to everyone. "Emerald, sweetheart, this is your grandfather, Clinton Washington." Emerald broke free of the detective's hand and ran to her grandfather. "Grand daddy!" she exclaimed as she hugged him so tightly he gasped for breath between his sobs of joy.

"And your grandmother, Sharon," said Detective Smith. Emerald hugged her grandmother and kissed her cheek.

"And your aunt, Shavon."

Emerald hugged Shavon and looked at them all in turn with her beautiful clear eyes. "But where's my daddy?"

And now, Lord, what wait I for?
My hope is in thee. Psalm 39:7

These wait all upon thee;
that thou mayest give them their
harvest in due season. Psalm 104:27

Shavon's day was over and she was back at home. She had a boring routine: work, church, and home. She hoped that would all change soon; she just had to wait. Waiting, for Shavon, was the hardest thing to do. God was giving her a lesson in patience, but she even wanted that to be over with as quickly as possible.

CHAPTER VII

PRAISE GOD FROM WHOM ALL BLESSINGS FLOW

Shavon returned home three days later to her regular routine. Her life was in sync again. It felt good being on familiar ground and enjoying life as she knew it.

When she returned to work, everything was going as planned. Maria handled the day-to-day operation of the office like a champ. Even some members of the board noticed and complimented her on a job well done. Shavon made a mental note to propose that Maria get a three percent raise once the annual budget was reviewed and allocated. Shavon had called Alana and Tarik and gave them a follow-up report on Emerald and Jasmine. They were both relieved that everything turned out for the good.

"Shavon, if you're planning to get Emerald over the summer, let me know so I can get my nieces, Paris and Shalom. We can make it a family affair!" Alana said. She was always good with children and loved any opportunity that allowed her to get her nieces. With her traveling all over Florida now, it was more difficult to spend any time with her little darlings.

"I do plan to get her. I'll let you know."

Shavon was ready to get back into the swing of things with work, church, and Travis. Shavon hadn't really chatted with him like she wanted to because she was trying to get settled.

There wasn't a day that she didn't think about him – Travis was constantly on her mind. She missed him so much while she was gone. Shavon was starting to feel guilty about her feelings for him. She didn't want to feel like a hypocrite. Though she was waiting for the Lord to send her a husband, she was also trying to help Him along.

The trip had set Shavon behind. She made herself a mental note of things she had to do. There was so much: she needed to call Pastor Dallas about the parking lot incident, email Travis, look through her budget reports, etc. Though her job kept her very busy, Shavon took pride in it. She didn't want to be considered a slacker by her staff or the board of directors.

Shavon called the church to schedule an appointment with Pastor Dallas. She was prepared to leave a message when an unfamiliar voice answered the phone: "God is good all the time and all the time God is good. Thank you for calling The Word Baptist Church where Pastor Dallas is the Pastor and Jesus Christ is Lord. How can we serve you?" Shavon was exhausted from just listening to her. The woman sounded so robotic, like she had been rehearsing that for six months straight with no interruptions.

Clearing her throat, Shavon replied, "This is Sister Shavon Washington. I would like to schedule an appointment with Pastor Dallas at his earliest convenience."

"What is this in reference to?" she snapped.

"It is in reference to a personal church matter," Shavon said.

"Look here, Honey," was her comeback, "the pastor is a very busy man, working on the battlefield for the Lord. I pray that it is important because neither the Lord nor the pastor have time for foolishness."

Shavon was going to have to pray for a super-sized portion of patience because she wanted to pull that sister's tongue out of her mouth with one jerk! "Ma'am, what date and time is he available because I am also very busy."

"Please hold while I check," she said.
Shavon knew that the woman was being mean and probably wanted her to hang up, so she didn't. She finally came back on the line. "My pastor is available for one hour and one hour only on June 8th at 2:00 pm."

"Thank you, ma'am; and remember that the Bible tells us to treat others as we want to be treated." Shavon could not believe that Pastor Dallas would have Satan's sister answering the church phone! She needed to get the anger she felt for her pastor out of her spirit. June 8th couldn't come soon enough.

Where does the time go? Shavon had to get to work and meet with the board of directors about hosting the Community Unity Ball this year. This year's ball is a black tie affair where community leaders, government officials, and civic and social groups come out for an elegant dinner to raise money for at-risk teens and their families. The event also includes a celebrity guest. This fundraiser was one that Ms. Spann hosted for years. It was her best fundraiser that helped keep the agency afloat each year. The event usually generated twenty to thirty thousand dollars in profits.

Shavon needed to meet with the board of directors to discuss the budget and nominations for this year's celebrity guest. She knew they needed to attract more minority guests than in years past and had to explain that to the board.

The board consisted of three Caucasian males, two Caucasian females, one African American female and one Hispanic male. Just as the board was culturally diverse, the Community Unity Ball needed to be just as diverse. Maria had picked up the PowerPoint presentation for Shavon from the copy center. She had an elaborate presentation for the board; she was going to woo them.

Maria was setting the scene to make them feel comfortable for the meeting; she had devised a plan to give them a sample of what the evening would be like so she called Catering Customs to help her with that task. She ordered a variety of specialty appetizers that reflected different cultures. She also ordered some homemade brownies and fresh baked cookies. Maria decorated the conference room in festive colors with music playing softly in the background to stimulate the board's imagination. She'd done a fantastic job and was truly a blessing to Shavon and the entire organization.

Shavon believed that God stationed her at her job to be Maria's 'guardian angel'. Sometimes, Shavon really didn't know what she'd do without Maria and her expertise. She had to give it to Maria – the girl was good.

Sonya, one of the at-risk case managers, was passing by the room on the way to the copier when she peeked her head in. She was amazed at how the room had been transformed.

"It's perfect!" Sonya exclaimed, feeling like she was at some elaborate party.

The scene was set. As Sonya passed Maria's desk, she gave her two thumbs up. Maria had a special gift, a unique touch. Last Christmas, Maria baked everyone two dozen of their favorite cookies and put them in hand-crafted tin containers with their names and a Bible verse. No one knew where Maria found the time or energy to be so thoughtful with four children and a husband.

Shavon went into the conference room and saw the preparations Maria had made. She was in complete shock. The conference room was transformed into a neat little ballroom. Shavon knew the board was going to be surprised and she was confident that everything would go fine. She praised God for all the help she'd received.

The board was impressed with Shavon's presentation. Each board member committed to buying or selling ten tickets at $150 each. The event was off to a good start already. Shavon knew it was the Lord that had given her the vision for this year's ball. Because it was from Him, she knew it would be a blessing for everyone involved and invited.

Shavon proposed the theme for this year's ball – Cultures Connecting: Hand in Hand. She believed it would help the youth's Hand in Hand program. Shavon spoke to them about having a calypso band for two hours, then a reggae band for an hour, followed by a DJ to play music from the 60s, 70s, and 80s. Further,

Shavon believed that having culturally-diverse foods would be a good idea. She even suggested that guests come dressed in attire to reflect their own ethnic backgrounds.

Dr. Carrington, the board's president, said: "That is a marvelous idea, Shavon. You're brilliant!" Dr. Carrington was the lead cardiologist at a major hospital in town. He'd gotten involved with the organization when his son, Sean, was killed by another teenage boy over a drug exchange that had gone wrong. Sean was going to buy marijuana from a known drug neighborhood when angry gang members became suspicious of him and thought he was a narc. The gang members beat him until he was unconscious. Hours later, he woke up and recognized Alton, a kid from school. That is when the gang decided to kill him. Alton, the newest member of the group, had to be the one to kill him. Alton didn't think he had much to live for, so he did it.

Dr. Carrington was so passionate about the organization's purpose that he soon became president. The amazing part of the story is that Dr. Carrington and his wife petitioned the state for the young man not to be sentenced to prison. They wanted to try to save another life since they couldn't save their own son. Dr. Carrington was granted the petition to adopt Alton, who is now a senior in college, majoring in youth and family services.

He wants to go back into the same community where that incident took place for him and try to make a difference. Talk about a success story, Alton and Dr. Carrington have one that is truly remarkable.

All that was left was deciding on a celebrity guest. Shavon didn't have a clue who she wanted to invite. The meeting was almost over, but she knew that question was going to be asked.

"Shavon, who will the celebrity guest be this year?"

"I have that covered. You will be notified soon."

The whole board applauded loudly. They were so happy. Everyone was confident that the Community Unity Ball was going to be a wonderful event. Shavon had a brief sense of relief but a bolt of lightning had entrapped her because she didn't have a lot of time to find a celebrity. She'd met a lot of people in her lifetime, but no one that could draw a huge crowd. Never mind the fact that she would be competing with Ms. Spann's stunning events from the past. At the last gala Ms. Spann hosted, Burt Reynolds was the celebrity guest. The board and older community leaders loved him. The youth didn't have a clue who he was, and thought he was on the 'corny' side. Still, it had been an overwhelming success in terms of turn out and money. There was no use in worrying herself sick over this. She was going to leave it up to the Lord. This was His vision; she was just a vessel helping to carry it out.

Shavon's day was over and she was back at home. She had a boring routine: work, church, and home. She hoped that would all change soon; she just had to wait. Waiting, for Shavon, was the hardest thing to do. God was giving her a lesson in patience, but she even wanted that to be over with as quickly as possible. But rather than focus on that, Shavon decided to focus on how well her day had gone. Everything was going good at work, and she and Maria had impressed the board. It had been a very productive day so she deserved a treat. No one else could do that for her; she decided that she was going to treat herself to a sweet delight. She got some vanilla ice cream to go with a pecan and walnut brownie. It was time to indulge! She was going to eat as much as she wanted and then go to bed. Well, maybe she'd email Travis first.

After pigging out, Shavon checked to see if Travis was online. She had to be honest with herself: she liked him a lot and that was scaring her a little bit. She found Travis online and they chatted until she got sleepy. She bade him farewell and got ready for bed. Then she remembered…"What on Earth am I going to wear to the ball?"

Shavon tried calling Alana several times. She needed some suggestions about where to shop for a dress. She wanted something spectacular, but classy. It couldn't just be any dress, so she didn't want to shop alone.

Shavon saw that the Billings' car was home. She still had their mail on her foyer table and needed to get it to them. She was praying they wouldn't look at the delivery date because it had been sitting at her house for at least two weeks. Only God knows how long it was in her mailbox. Shavon put on her slides and walked across the street. Jeff and Gina Billings and their two sons, Timothy (age eight) and Brendon (age three), were home and luckily, still up. She hated to disturb them.

In fact, when she first moved into her house, the Billings were the first neighbors to come over and welcome her to the Madison Gardens subdivision. She remembered it like it was yesterday, particularly the look on Mrs. Billings' face when she found out that Shavon was single. I guess she couldn't figure out how a single, young African American woman could afford a Mercedes and a $200,000 house. Truth is, it was a God thing. "Praise God from whom all blessings flow!" According to Romans 8:31, if God is for you, who can be against you? God had promised her that if she remained faithful to Him, He was going to give her the desires of her heart. He had kept all of His promises.

When she approached the Billings' home, she could hear some verbal commotion going on. She slipped the mail under a flowerpot that was on their porch and tip-toed away. She was actually glad they weren't available because she wasn't in the mood for small talk. Though she did want to invite them to the ball, she could do that at any time.

Back home, Shavon took her shower and got into bed with her laptop. Just as she was about to sign into her email, the phone rang. She hoped it was Travis, but the caller ID read Clinton Washington. Shavon's day had been almost perfect and she didn't want it ruined.

"Hello?" she answered.

"Shavon!" her mother's voice came back. Shavon could hear the excitement in her mother's voice. "I have some wonderful news to tell you."

Shavon hadn't heard her mother sound so excited in years, not since her father had surprised her with a seven-day cruise to Hawaii.

"What, Mama? Tell me."

"Clayson has been offered two jobs in one day!" Shavon bowed her head and lifted her hands to the Lord. "Hallelujah!"

Apparently, Clayson had come over to the house to get Emerald and take her to the mall for the day. That was normal because he got Emerald every other weekend, came to see her at least four days a week, and called every day that she wasn't with him. Shavon's mother explained that while they were at the mall, a modeling scout from Global Enterprise saw Clayson and Emerald together and asked him if Emerald had ever modeled.

Clayson was apprehensive about talking to a complete stranger about his daughter. He didn't know if the man was legitimate or not. Clayson tried to brush him off but he was too adamant. The man asked him if he could buy them lunch at the Cheesecake Factory restaurant and discuss some opportunities.

The man said that Emerald was the most beautiful young girl he'd seen. He was convinced that Emerald had a look that America needed to see. Clayson was still very skeptical but was willing to listen. Clayson asked if he could have a few minutes to talk this over with his daughter. Clayson asked Emerald if she was interested in having lunch with this man who wanted to talk to them about a modeling opportunity. Of course, she was ecstatic!

"Daddy, you know my mama said I was going to be a model some day, and she was right. I can't wait to tell her!"

Shavon was proud of Clayson. Ever since Emerald had come back into his life, he was moving and growing by leaps and bounds. The depression had disappeared. From what Shavon could decipher, while they were eating lunch and discussing how to make modeling a reality for Emerald, the man asked Clayson if he'd ever modeled before. The answer was no, but he had taken a few photos for Sports Illustrated while playing college and professional football. The man thought for a little while and then remembered Clayson. He couldn't believe it!

"Are you the Clayson Washington?"

"Yes, that would be me."

Clayson then found out that the man was also affiliated with the National Fitness for Life Youth Coalition. The NFLYC was a campaign sponsored by the President and his Cabinet to advocate for fitness around the world and to fight the national child obesity problem. The President was trying to steer youth to stay away from fatty foods and participate more in physical fitness programs.

"We need someone like you to be the face and spokesperson for this movement, Mr. Washington," the man said.

Emerald sat quietly for as long as she could stand it. Finally, she had to say something. "Excuse me, sir, but where do I fit into this?"Both Clayson and the man chuckled. "You're definitely in the forefront sweetheart; we are going to use you as the poster child. By the way, my name is Thaddeus Swartz."

"Nice to get your name, Mr. Swartz," Clayson said.

"We have been looking for the right face, a role model, if you will. I think I've found my man."

Shavon's mom said Mr. Swartz offered Clayson a $1.5 million annual contract with a $150,000 sign-on bonus that would pay for his role in the campaign, a modeling contract for both him and Emerald, and free trips around the world to be that organization's spokesperson.

Clayson was nervous and sweating profusely. His prayer for God to restore everything he'd lost seemed to happen suddenly. It was similar to the story of Job in the Bible. He'd lost it all, and now it was being multiplied back to him in a double-fold.

Clayson asked Mr. Swartz to give him a few minutes to think this over – he needed to pray first.

After Mr. Swartz left the table, Clayson said a short prayer, asking God for direction. He couldn't afford to make any more mistakes, particularly where Emerald was concerned. Shavon's mom went on to tell her about Clayson's mysterious text message behind the prayer for direction – it was truly amazing. As Clayson finished praying, his phone vibrated. It was a text message from an unfamiliar number. When he opened the phone, there was a text that read, "Son, I got your call, and it is okay. I'll talk with you soon." Clayson was overcome with emotions. He began to sob at the goodness of God. God was surely with him and he knew it. Emerald had never seen her father so emotional. She climbed on his lap and planted a huge kiss on his cheek. "Daddy, you're the best daddy in the world!"

After Mr. Swartz returned, Clayson agreed to take the offer with one stipulation: Emerald had to be able to travel with him. Mr. Swartz did him one better and promised to arrange for a certified home school teacher to travel with them also. They exchanged numbers and it was a done deal.

Shavon was very happy for Clayson. She began to cry as her mother told her the story. It was just further proof of God's goodness and faithfulness. He'd answered Clayson's prayers and the prayers of their entire family for him. Before Shavon's mother got off the phone, because she had more family to call, she had one more bit of good news: Shavon's father had received a clean bill of health from his doctor.

Hallelujah! More answered prayers. Shavon had been professing healing over her father's life and the whole family was rebuking prostate cancer.

Shavon got off the phone and logged on to the internet; she needed to talk to Travis again. Sure enough, he was there. It was as if he knew she'd be logging on. Shavon was in a playful mood after all of the praise reports.

"Hello, My Black Emperor. I found out where you live and I'm on my way over."

"Sorry, I was just about to go to bed," he immediately replied. "I have an early meeting tomorrow. But I'm so glad that you thought enough to check on me. LOL!"

"Can I confess something to you?" Shavon said boldly.

"Yes, as long as you don't tell me you're really a man. LOL!" he joked.

"Well, you're lucky. I happen to be a very attractive young woman!" she said.

"Yes, I already know that you're a young woman with a trillion-dollar personality," he responded. Shavon blushed. Travis always said the right things. Shavon had to share her day with Travis.

"Travis, would it be alright if I logged off and called you?"

"Sure. Hurry up because I'm dying to hear your voice!"

There was a lot going on in Shavon's mind and heart concerning Travis. She found herself constantly fighting against conflicting emotions. She wanted to see him, but she knew neither of them were ready for that stage of the relationship. Chatting online had to be enough for now.

So she called him; and after talking Travis' head off about Clayson, Emerald, the ball and work, she realized that she'd nearly put him to sleep without giving him even a moment to share his day with her. But since they both had to get up early, they called it a night. Neither of them wanted to get off the phone, but they each had a lot of responsibility.

After hanging up, Travis stared at the phone and whispered, "Shavon Washington, you are going to be my wife one day. I can feel it."

Shavon laid her head on her pillow and prayed: "Father, I hope you hear me. I'm falling in love with Travis and I'm afraid of making a mistake. If he will be my husband, please show me soon. Thank you for my job and for Maria. I love you, Father. Amen."

Shavon got into bed. About the time she was getting settled in, the phone rang. It was Travis. "Shavon, I know we said goodbye, but turn to ESPN. Good night."

Just that quickly, he'd hung up. Shavon grabbed her remote and turned her television to ESPN. She caught a glimpse of what looked like Clayson. She turned up the volume and heard the commentator say, "He's back and stronger than ever. Clayson Washington has been named as the spokesperson for the President's National Fitness for Life Youth Coalition."

Shavon sat straight up in the bed. She'd found her celebrity guest for the Community Unity Ball; it was going to be her brother, Clayson Demetrius Washington! All Shavon could do was praise God. It was ridiculous how wonderful God was blessing them. All she had to do was get a commitment from him. Shavon was dancing all over her bedroom. Go Clayson! Go Jesus! Go Clayson! Go Jesus!

Shavon could hardly believe she just said that, it just sort of oozed out of her heart. Shavon had developed some feelings for Travis, but she knew that she had to move forward in this relationship with caution. Shavon began to think about how she was twenty-seven years old, wasn't married, and didn't have any children. She had a wonderful life, but not really anyone to share it with...

CHAPTER VIII

A HEART TO HELP

Shavon was on cloud nine all day and walked with an extra pep in her step. She had a glow that brightened up the whole office; everyone could tell she was in a joyous mood. Shavon was listening to the gospel radio station in her office when Diane, the HR Director, tapped on the door. "May I speak with you briefly? It's a personal matter."

It was obvious that Diane was upset about something. She was normally a very reserved person. She rarely said anything; but when she did, it was heard by everyone. Diane was very soft-spoken and seldom socialized on the job. Her philosophy was that she came to work to fulfill an assignment; she didn't come for a social gathering. If Diane needed to talk with her, it had to be quite serious.

"How can I help?" Shavon asked.

"Well, I really need a six-week leave of absence. My husband and I are having problems and it has gotten to the point where it is affecting my work here and I don't want that to happen," Diane replied.

Diane had been married for about eight years. She and her husband had a five-year-old son named Eden. About nine months ago, Diane found out her husband Phillip was abusing cocaine. She thought he had been having an affair because of the hours he kept and that he was giving some woman his money because it was disappearing quickly, but it was actually a drug addiction. Phillip started suffering from severe mood swings; and Diane got the shock of her life when a thug showed up at their house at 3 am one morning, demanding that Phillip give him the $500 he owed him for drugs.

Diane decided to stay with him and try to help him through it, but it was a lot harder than it seemed. Phillip finally signed up for an outpatient substance abuse program; but apparently after the third visit, he decided to stop going. He then lost his job of twelve years as a car salesman because of his lack of attendance and some accusations of petty theft.

"Ms. Washington, I really need some time to decide what I'm going to do. I have to think of my son." Diane looked like she'd aged five years in a matter of minutes. Though she was a strong woman, this was getting the better of her. She normally was the picture of strength, but it was obvious that she was struggling.

Shavon gave Diane a big hug. Her heart went out to her; it couldn't possibly be easy. "I can arrange for you to work from home with payroll. You will need to come into the office about once a week and keep up with your emails."

"Thank you so much. I appreciate this. I will definitely do a good job," Diane said with a sigh of relief.

"Great! Can I help you with anything else?" asked Shavon.

"You can pray for me and my family," she replied.

"Consider it done," said Shavon. "Now remember to get me the information that you normally use for employee benefits as I may have to fill in for you."

Before Diane left, Shavon grabbed her hand and prayed: "Father, I come before you today, asking you to look upon Diane and her family. I know that you have seen the hurt that my sister Diane has had to endure. Father, I ask you to give her strength to sustain her until you deliver her husband Phillip from cocaine and restore him as the husband and father you have called him to be. Father, heal this family's pain. Father, shield Diane and Phillip's seed, Eden, from any confusion he may be feeling. Lord, you are a God of peace and love and I pray that you overshadow Diane with your love in her time of despair. Lord, Diane and Phillip are your children and they need you right now! Amen."

Shavon gave Diane's hand a tight squeeze and walked her towards the door. Diane felt better already. She needed an inspirational touch from the Lord and she needed it right now. Once Diane left, Shavon's heart was sore. She could feel Diane's pain. Shavon had a heart for people and wanted to accommodate Diane to the best of her ability. Shavon was going to call Maria into her office and inform her that the board of directors had approved the Community Unity Ball as well as having granted her a three percent raise that would be effective on her next paycheck. She was also going to ask her if she would be available to assist her as Diane would be away for six weeks.

Shavon regained her composure after talking with Diane and called Maria into the office. Maria arrived in less than two minutes with a pen and legal pad in hand ready to take notes. Maria looked good; she had been losing weight and it was noticeable today. Maria rarely wore any makeup, but today she had on a little lip gloss and eyeliner. Shavon could tell she had gotten her eyebrows arched because it complemented her face well.

As Maria sat down, Shavon asked if she could fill in as needed because Diane was going to have to take off a few weeks for personal reasons. Maria smiled and said: "Yes, I can do anything to keep this organization afloat." Maria had such a positive attitude and it was contagious; there had been times when people in the office mentioned having a bad day; but after talking with Maria, they felt so much better.

Shavon then told Maria that she had been approved by the board for a three percent raise. Maria was speechless and turned Christmas-bulb red. She started to cry tears of joy and couldn't even speak except to praise God. After getting herself together, she told Shavon that she had been asking God to enlarge her territory. She even had the Jabez prayer as her screensaver. She didn't know it would come so soon. Maria said that she and her husband wanted to become homeowners but were advised by the mortgage company that they needed at least a few hundred dollars more of net income a month to qualify for a four-bedroom, two and one half bath home.

Shavon thought if anybody needed a chance at home ownership, it was Maria and her family. When Maria came to work for the organization, she and her husband and three of the children were living with her husband's parents in a three bedroom house. Maria often talked of moving into their own place. When they were able to move into a two-bedroom apartment, Maria was so excited. Then she set her vision on a home; and now with the raise, her dream would finally come true.

Maria asked Shavon about the ball. Shavon knew that she needed to get started on planning for the big event; she had less than three months to get everything planned as the event was scheduled for August 6th. Shavon didn't want to place the horse before the cart, so she decided not to tell anyone about the celebrity guest until it was confirmed.

Shavon mentioned to Maria that she was going to work on the ball and that Maria should screen all of her calls until 4:00.

Shavon took her cell phone from her purse to find Clayson's phone number and gave him a call. Shavon was hoping that Clayson had not changed his number again. To her recollection, he had changed his number at least twelve times within the last three years! Shavon dialed the number and, for some reason, she felt nervous and nauseous at the same time. On the third ring, Emerald answered the phone. "Hello, this is Emerald, how can my daddy help you?" Emerald was so cute; she had really lit a spark under her daddy.

"Emerald, this is Auntie Shavon, how are you doing?" she asked.

Emerald screeched, "Auntie Shavon, "Where is your daddy, Emerald?" inquired Shavon.

"He is standing right here," Emerald replied.

Clayson took the phone from Emerald and sounding like he was sitting on top of the world said, "Hi, Lil Sis. How are you? I've been meaning to call you to thank you for seeing about Emerald and making my life complete again."

"Clayson, it was all God and His divine plan for your life," Shavon rebutted.

"Amen, Sis, Amen!" Clayson said. "How is everything in Gator Nation?"

"All is well in 'Titleville'. With the basketball team and the football team winning national titles, it has been crazy in this town." Even though she was still an avid Gator fan, she had not been to any sporting events in about two years. “Clayson, Mama told me about your new career opportunities and I'm so proud of you!”

“Yes, God is so good,” he said. “I don’t have anything to complain about. I wasn't even looking for a blessing; yet out of nowhere, one showed up.”

“You know, that is just how God works.” Shavon replied.

Clayson went on to share with her how he was just walking through the mall with Emerald trying to find her a bathing suit for the summer while his blessing was lurking around the corner. Shavon thought of the reason she was calling Clayson in the first place; maybe this was a good time to ask him for a big favor. Shavon knew Clayson had never been able to tell her "no" before and she didn’t think he would tell her "no" now. Shavon didn’t know why, but she was nervous about it.

Shavon had not been this nervous since the time she was in the 11th grade and wanted to ask Clayson, together with a couple of friends, to rent an Expedition limousine and get a suite at the Carlton for the prom. Shavon had finally stored up her courage and asked him; and within 24 hours, the arrangements had been made and she had confirmation numbers to prove it.

Clayson was so generous with everyone; he would help anyone. This was the reason he had been so hurt after his football injury. He had felt that the whole world had turned against him, including the people he had helped in the past. Clayson donated to almost every charity in Miami; and when he would encounter some of his more unfortunate classmates, he would bless them with a few hundred dollars.

Shavon felt her nerves settle a bit, so she took the plunge and said, "Clayson, I am hosting a Community Unity Ball for my organization. I would really appreciate it if you would be our celebrity guest."

"Oh Shavon, I would be absolutely honored to!" Clayson replied.

Shavon went on to inform him that the event was scheduled for August 6th. She asked him to contact his agent to double check that he was not already booked for that same date. Clayson responded, "If I am, then I will have to change it because family always comes first in my book – especially you." Shavon asked him to call her ASAP to confirm once he had talked with his agent. Clayson told her it was as good as done. Shavon was so thankful that Clayson was available; she knew immediately within her spirit that the Community Unity Ball was going to be a huge success.

"Clayson, has Emerald heard from Jasmine?" Shavon asked.

"She wrote a letter to Emerald last week and ever since, Emerald has been asking about going to see her." Clayson had told her that he would take her when she was ready as Jasmine was in a Metropolitan Correctional Center in New York for women. Shavon and Clayson finished their call, both promising to remain in touch as things happened.

After hanging up, Shavon recalled her mother saying that Jasmine had been sentenced to three years' prison time and 10 years' probation. Shavon's parents had been awarded joint custody with Clayson. Emerald was happy to be spending time with them, but everyone knew she missed her mother. The family had decided they would respect that as long as she was in their lives, which was going to be forever.

Shavon stood up and did her little praise dance, 'getting her shout on'. Her mind then drifted back to Diane. Shavon wanted to send her a love token so she called Al's Flower Shop down the street and ordered a bouquet of spring flowers, asking that they be delivered by 4 pm. Shavon wanted Diane to know that she cared.

Shavon took out her legal pad and started making a list of possible places to host the ball. Over the years, it had been at the Women's Club, University Central Hotel, and The Marriot Grand Ball Room. Shavon wanted this year's ball to be an elegant, yet friendly and inviting event for all in attendance. Shavon decided to call an event planner and get some advice. Although Shavon knew how she wanted the event to be, she just needed a boost in finalizing the plans in her mind. She went online and searched the web for local event planners, finding three that seemed to specialize in corporate events. As she was very impressed with Events Planned by Kandra Albury, Shavon forwarded the Internet links over to Maria and asked her to schedule an appointment with them within the next two weeks.

While Shavon was already on the computer, she decided to check her email. There was a lot of junk mail, but there were two emails from Alana, one with 'ESPN' as the subject. Shavon watched. In this piece, Clayson was being interviewed by ESPN about his national debut with the youth and fitness organization. At the end, they showed a picture of him and Emerald working out at the local YMCA gym. Emerald looked so cute in her purple Nike outfit. Shavon had not seen much television in the last couple of weeks so she hadn't seen the interview. Shavon replied to the email, "I'm so proud of Clayson; I'll share details later."

The second email was a joke about how to tell the difference between a dog and a man. Shavon closed the message, thinking that she would read that one much later.

The third email was pictures of Michelle O'Bama and her interview with Barbara Walters.

Shavon decided to see if Travis was online. She remembered he said that he had an important meeting to attend this morning. She was wondering if he was finished; she wanted to talk with him. Shavon logged on to the site and Mr. Black Emperor was in idle mode as usual; it was if he was always waiting for an opportunity to talk with her, so he just stayed logged on just in case she wanted to chat.

Shavon wrote, "I can hardly wait until tonight; just wanted to say hi."

Travis immediately responded, "I'm glad you couldn't wait because I have been thinking about you since last night."

Shavon smiled to herself and typed, "I have so much to tell you."

Travis blushed and wrote back, "I am dying to hear it!"

Since Shavon did not know when a good time would be to call Travis, she wrote, "What would be a good time to call you tonight?"

He replied, "Anytime after 7:00".

Shavon responded, "Great, I will call you."

Taking a deep breath for courage and deciding not to hesitate, she continued, "I was hoping that we could take our conversation to another level." And then she logged off.

Shavon could hardly believe she just said that; it just sort of oozed out of her heart. Shavon had developed some feelings for Travis, but she knew that she had to move forward in this relationship with caution. Shavon began to think about how she was twenty-seven years old, wasn't married, and didn't have any children. She had a wonderful life, but not really anyone to share it with. Shavon had thought that she and Kenneth would have been happily married, but that fantasy soon came to a halt after he lost his desire to be dedicated. Since then, she had to admit that she had endured some lonely days and restless nights. It was her faith that helped her make it through the rough times.

While Shavon was sitting there reviewing the 'tapes' of her life, she looked at the clock and noticed it was now 4:07 pm. Maria buzzed in, "You have three phone messages and there is a Mo'keisha in the lobby to see you." Shavon wondered what Mo wanted and replied to Maria, "Please have Mo'keisha come back to my office and bring the phone messages with you."

Mo was talking so loudly coming down the hallway that Shavon could hear her voice bouncing off the walls – Mo's pitch was way too high for indoors. She evidently had not learned the skill of using an inside voice. Mo was not completely in the doorframe when she blurted out, "Vonny girl, I didn't know you had it like this! Got your name on the door and everything. Girl, you're doing it big!"

With a little smirk on her face, Maria handed Shavon the messages and closed the door. Shavon surveyed the messages quickly noting that one was from Alana and the other from Clayson.

Mo was still in shock, looking all around the office before finally saying, "Vonny girl, I knew you had a good job, but I didn't know you were 'the boss' – I could've gotten a job here! Oh yeah, Vonny, I came by to give you the money I borrowed. Vonny, you are going to be so proud of me; I have all the money this time."

Shavon felt her heart tighten up: Mo had never paid her back on time or in full before. Shavon knew she usually had to wait until income tax time to be paid. Mo went on to tell her she had been playing bingo and luck was on her side. Shavon knew how obsessive compulsive Mo could be; she hoped this wouldn't become an addiction. Mo blurted out, "Yeah Vonny, you didn't tell me that Clayson Washington was your brother. I saw his fine self on TV the other night with a cute little girl."

Shavon just laughed and said. "Yes, Clayson is my brother and the little girl is my niece, Emerald."

Mo replied, "Girl, where is that little girl's mama? Ask him if she needs a step-mama." Shavon was listening to Mo go on and on but she knew Clayson didn't need any more drama in his life for a while, so she did not reply to Mo's questions.

Mo finally said that she had to go and pick up Jaheem and Destiny from aftercare and Tyra from daycare. Shavon thanked Mo for paying her back and placed the money in her desk drawer because she knew Mo would be back to borrow it again within the next thirty days.

It was now after 5 pm and everyone was gone except Shavon and Diane. Diane stopped by Shavon's office with her flowers and a few files and said, "Shavon, thank you again for everything. God bless you!"

Shavon told Diane to call her anytime, even if she just needed someone to talk to. Diane said, "I have your numbers in my cell phone. Thank you for the offer."

Shavon said, "Diane, remember there is nothing too hard for God."

Diane just nodded her head and walked off. Shavon started gathering her things to leave when she saw a dark shadow walk across her door. Shavon grabbed her car and office keys and called out to Diane, but she did not get an answer. Shavon then called out to Maria; and again, no answer.

Shavon didn't think anyone else was still in the building; at least she did not see anyone. When she was about to push the elevator button, she heard another sound and, to her relief, it was Mr. Clyde, the night custodian.

Mr. Clyde apologized saying, "Sorry, Ms. Washington. I didn't mean to scare you." He continued, "I am working a little late this whole week to get in a few extra hours so I can buy my wife an anniversary gift. It is going to be our 21st wedding anniversary. I submitted it to Ms. Diane last week. You will probably get the request if you haven't already." Mr. Clyde had been with the agency for about 25 years. He was a very hard worker and hadn't missed a day of work in all that time.

Shavon asked him, "So, when is your wedding anniversary?" Mr. Clyde responded by saying, tomorrow. Shavon just smiled, "Mr. Clyde, I left something in my office for you, do you mind waiting with me?"

Mr. Clyde had no idea what she was up to, but he had hope shining in his eyes and said yes without hesitation. When Shavon reached her office she went inside and retrieved the hundred dollars that Mo had brought by. Shavon then left her office where Mr. Clyde was standing and said to him, "Mr. Clyde, take this and use it to take your wife out to dinner tomorrow night, and you can have tonight off as well."

Mr. Clyde opened his hand, surprised to see a crisp one hundred-dollar bill. Shavon said, "Have a good night with your wife and I will still authorize your overtime." Giving him a small peck on the cheek, she motioned to leave the building but Mr. Clyde was about blown off his feet. He finally replied to her, "Thank you, Ms. Washington! God bless you! No one has ever blessed me like this before." He went on, "I'll be sure to pay you back with my next paycheck."

"No, Mr. Clyde," Shavon replied. "Consider this a blessing that is yours to keep."

Mr. Clyde was silent as they rode the elevator down to the lobby. Shavon glanced at him and noticed his eyes were shining with unshed tears and he had a huge grin on his face. Once they reached the lobby after having exited the elevator, Mr. Amos, the security officer on duty, said, "Goodnight Ms. Washington and Mr. Clyde."

They both replied, "Goodnight, Mr. Amos" while leaving the building.

Driving home, Shavon remembered that she had no food worth eating at home and decided to stop by Publix and pick up a few items. She had intended to just pick up a few things, but she ended up getting eighty-six dollars worth of groceries.

Shavon hated it when she went into the grocery store hungry; she always overspent.

Shavon was ready to go home. She wanted to shower and get ready for her phone date with Travis. She was having pre-date jitters: smiling, feeling mushy inside, and humming to herself. She was just happy for no apparent reason other than she was going to be talking with Travis Elliot soon, very soon.

When she pulled into the driveway, she noticed the yardman had been there; she had forgotten to leave his check under the flower pot as she had been doing for the last couple of years. Shavon knew she needed to call him and apologize. She lifted all of the grocery bags out of the car and put them away. Shavon didn't like lugging groceries; at least when Kenneth was around, he would do this much for her. She had found the one thing that Kenneth was good at – Wow!

Shavon decided that for supper she would have baked tilapia coated with bread crumbs and a Greek salad. Shavon hadn't eaten any lunch; she had only drank a V-8 Splash around one o'clock but that was it. Shavon washed her hands, slung off her shoes and prepped her fish; preheating the oven on broil. She then headed for the shower. Shavon felt good that she was able to help Mr. Clyde and Diane today. She knew that God was pleased. Shavon was a cheerful giver, like in Second Corinthians 9:7; she loved helping others. What made her the happiest was seeing others happy.

Shavon returned to the kitchen, having finished her shower. She finished cooking her dinner and sat down to eat; it was delicious, especially since she had been very hungry. Shavon figured she needed to cook more often because when God sent her a husband, she was not going to be a 'menu wife', always going out to eat. She made up her mind she was going to become more familiar with her stove so that she would be prepared to cook for her husband when God sent her one. Shavon had seen how her own mother would cook and clean, and she had heard her aunt, Deloris, say personally that a man liked a clean house and a hearty meal on the table when he got home. She knew she wouldn't have a problem cleaning, but she was going to have to work on the cooking part.

Shavon called Mr. Henry, the yardman, and got his voicemail. Mr. Henry was a funny man; he had the same voicemail message for years. Mr. Henry was about 70 years old and did a splendid job. He said that he used to let his great-grandsons work with him, but they started slowing him down by wanting to take too many breaks and complaining all the time. Mr. Henry said he was going to go with the old saying: "If you want something done right, then do it yourself." So he now worked alone.

Shavon was anxious about her cyber date with Travis. She had even put on a dab or two of lip gloss and put her hair in a nice flowing ponytail. She knew he wouldn't be able to see her, but she wanted to feel the part. It wasn't quite time for her and Travis to connect so she turned on the TV; and after flicking through the channels and finding nothing, she turned it off.

Shavon grabbed her cell phone and called Alana. She couldn't remember her schedule so she called her home number. Drayton, Alana's boyfriend, answered on the second ring. Drayton said Alana wasn't home, but he would let her know that Shavon had called. Shavon felt that Drayton could be a little dry sometimes, so she made a mental note to check back in with Alana to make sure everything was going okay with them these days; maybe the long hours Alana was working was starting to affect Drayton. Shavon knew that no man wanted to be home alone all the time.

Shavon still had a few minutes until she was to have her phone date with Travis. She was acting like it was a real date. It was 6:57 pm and she was anxious. She went to the kitchen to make sure that she had cleaned up behind herself because she didn't want to face that in the morning. It was now 8:07 pm and he still had not called. Shavon figured that maybe she would just call him to check on him and see if by chance he had forgotten. She called his home and the phone just rang and rang until on the fourth ring, his answering machine picked up so she left a message. Shavon was disappointed – she had been stood up on a phone date and felt like a fool! Shavon tried to think realistically, but a part of her wanted to say that she had been duped once again. Shavon was trying to trust Travis, but there were some inconsistencies in his stories about this friend of his that he was spending time with. Could this friend be a female friend? Shavon had not asked. Shavon had trouble with Kenneth when he started neglecting their relationship, and she could no longer ignore the signs Travis was sending. She was being gullible and she didn't like it.

She had hoped that this would be a love match in the making, but she was feeling doubtful and that was not good. She was trying to be optimistic and not read too much into the situation, but something was warning her that he was not the 'Emperor' she had previously hoped and prayed he would be.

Shavon finally heard from Travis the following morning about 7:45. He called and said that he was at a friend's house and that he was going through a crisis. He was trying to be supportive of his friend as the friend had been a mentor to him when they had met a couple of years ago. As a result, Travis did not feel he could just leave his friend in the state they had been in, thereby missing their phone date that night. Travis concluded by saying he hoped that Shavon would forgive him. She just sat on the phone listening. She didn't say a word at all. Travis was thinking that Shavon wasn't listening to a word he was saying and it was starting to irritate him a little bit. Shavon finally replied, "Okay, Travis. Thank you for calling, but I have to get into the office. Maybe we can reschedule our date you missed."

Hanging up from talking with Travis, Shavon didn't know if she should believe his story or not; she knew things can happen, but what about calling to cancel or was that forbidden in the cyber dating world? Shavon needed to consult the one person who would know what to do in a situation like this, so she called on Jesus. She fell to her knees on the side of her bed and said, "Lord, I'm going to have to be real with you. I'm falling for this guy, Travis; but right now I'm feeling like he is not telling me the truth. Lord you are going to have to be real with me. What should I do? Lord, did I mention that he stood me up on a cyber date?"

Shavon heard the Lord say in her spirit, "My child, the advice that I have for you is wait on me to reveal to you the desires of your heart."

For we through the Spirit wait
for the hope of righteousness
by faith. Galatians 5:5

She fell to her knees and prayed. Shavon was going to have straight talk with her heavenly father tonight. She was falling for Travis and while it was exhilarating, it also scared her. Shavon prayed for God to reveal if Travis was the one for her. She wanted to know if he was to be her "husband"...

CHAPTER XI

SAY AMEN

Today was June 8th; it was a very important day for Shavon. She was scheduled for an appointment with Pastor Dallas at 2 pm. She wanted to make sure that she didn't miss this appointment. Shavon started to think that Pastor Dallas had forgotten about having her car towed and she didn't want to appear psychotic about the whole ordeal. It had been over a month since she had even been to church. With everything going on, Shavon had not been to church, and for her that was awkward. Shavon knew Sister Karen had probably crossed her name off the choir roll. She wanted to call Sister Karen and explain her absence but she knew Sister Karen didn't take any excuses.

Shavon got up extra early; she wanted to get off to a good start this morning. She said Psalm 118:24 out loud, to create the right atmosphere.

"This is the day the Lord has made, let us rejoice and be glad in it." She smiled.

Shavon put in her "Shekinah Glory" CD and skipped ahead to the song called "Yes", which she loved. It gave her assurance that God was in control. While the song was playing, Shavon chose to wear something very conservative to show that she was not a disgruntled 'church hood rat'. She was ready for work in less than an hour, which was record time for her as she usually lagged around if she really didn't have much to do. She would watch Creflo Dollar or Paula White before leaving the house. Shavon really liked listening to Pastor Dollar because he always had a funny story to tell that related to his sermon. She had a few minutes to spare, so she decided to swing by Starbucks to get a caramel latte and a toasted bagel with garden cream cheese.

Shavon thought about her last conversation with Travis, trying to determine if he was being honest with her or not. She really wanted to believe him, but she had also wanted to believe Kenneth at the time when she should have followed her gut feeling instead.

At 9 am, Maria was not at her desk. Maria was always at work by 8:30 am and if by chance she was running late, she would always call ahead and let someone know she would be a few extra minutes or so. Shavon didn't remember seeing her mini-van in the parking lot and hoped that everything was okay. Shavon roamed the halls to see who she could find – she found Rose.

Rose was the case manager supervisor who had been with the organization for about twelve years. Rose had been Ms. Spann's right-hand woman, and she was very bitter when Shavon took Ms. Spann's place. She assumed she would get the position of program director. Rose had not been offered the job because she lacked the educational requirements. The board of directors liked Rose, but she was voted against, six to one.

Since that decision, Rose began to treat Shavon very coldly. However, Shavon always warmed her up with kindness. Shavon was determined she would turn the other cheek every time Rose slapped her with an evil look or a crude word. Rose tried almost every tactic in the book to get the board to fire Shavon. Rose did a remarkable job and Shavon liked her assertiveness and her productivity. Rose was a very good supervisor; she made sure that the case managers were all in compliance with policies and procedures and she kept the organization out of the trouble zone when it came to audits.

What upset Rose was that Shavon had told her she would petition for her raise by July 20th when the budget was allocated on August 1st. On August 2nd, Rose filed a grievance with the board alleging that Shavon had breached a verbal contract and she wanted to see immediate action taken against her. The board knew that there was no substance to her complaint so they all voted against her petition and denied her raise. Rose, however, never said anything to Shavon but her actions toward her spoke louder than words.

Shavon went into her office and noticed that her voicemail light was blinking. It looked like a red flashing Christmas light. Shavon put her briefcase and purse away before checking the message. There were three voicemails and all three were from Maria calling to let Shavon know that she wasn't coming in because she had to take her youngest child, Ricardo, to the doctor as he had been battling with a high fever all night. Maria was a very good mother. She rarely took off, even when the kids were sick. She would work half a day, while her husband stayed home and they switched so he could go to work.

Maria's message said that she had tried to call Shavon's cell phone but had not gotten an answer. Shavon had forgotten to charge up her cell phone; it was probably completely dead by now. Shavon would have to charge the phone once she got home because she didn't have a charger at work. Shavon thumbed through her day planner. She had two appointments scheduled for today: a 10:15 am meeting at the United Way for a non-profit executive community forum meeting and a 2 pm appointment with Pastor Dallas. The United Way usually hosted a quarterly meeting for all non-profit organizations, especially the ones that received some sort of funding from them. The meeting was an opportunity to share any agency updates. Shavon was going to disclose information about the Community Unity Ball. She was going to try to solicit a few ticket sales. Shavon enjoyed going to these quarterly meetings because she always came away with some very good ideas and updated information to share with her staff.

She was anxious about finally coming face to face with Pastor Dallas. She also knew that she would have to go through 'Satan's Sister' to even speak with him, but she was prayed up and had on her full armor of God, so she felt prepared. She was ready for battle. Sitting in United Way's forum meeting, Shavon didn't really want to think about that meeting as her mind was still on Travis.

Shavon couldn't believe that he had stood her up for their cyber date. Shavon wondered how a person got dumped for a cyber date, of all things! Shavon felt Travis could be telling the truth but she didn't know him from Adams' house cat, so why should she believe him? She had always read in the Bible to put your trust in no man, so why should she trust Travis?

Shavon heard the forum facilitator say, "Shavon Washington, would you like to share?"

With Shavon in the middle of questioning herself about Travis and the issue of trust, she was totally caught off guard but gathered herself quickly. Clearing her throat she replied, "Yes, we are hosting our Unity Ball on August 6th from 7 pm until 12 midnight. Our theme is Cultures Connecting: Hand in Hand." Shavon looked around the room and there were eyes of amazement found all around. Shavon continued, "We will have a vast array of different cultural music, food, and other entertainment. The tickets are $150 each. The funds collected will be used for college scholarships and other mentoring opportunities in our area." With much pride, Shavon also mentioned their celebrity guest would be Clayson Washington, former Miami Hurricane and Pittsburgh Steelers all-time record-holding quarterback.

An older gentleman said, "I saw a promo on television last night about him and his drive to overcome a major injury and how he is back full force as the spokesperson for the President's National Fitness for Life Youth Coalition and was campaigning with his daughter Diamond."

Shavon gently corrected the man, "Actually, Sir, her name is Emerald."

The man replied, "I knew it was some sort of gemstone."

A young intern whom Shavon thought was too observant said, "So, Ms. Washington, is Clayson your husband? I see you share the same last name."

Shavon could very easily have added some spice to her reply by saying something about having slept in the same bed with him before, but she did not let the devil use her. She instead just said, "Clayson is my older brother and I am honored to have him as our celebrity guest."

There was a young intern sitting in the front row with B. B. B. S. embroidered on her pink polo shirt who sat straight up in her chair at that announcement and said, "Ms. Washington, I'll take 20 tickets for me and my sorority sisters. We love Clayson Washington, he is so hot!" We think what he is doing is awesome. The whole room just laughed and Shavon smiled and said, "Thank you. I will get your contact information right after the meeting." The forum committee sponsored a small brunch and Shavon grabbed a cup of assorted tropical fruit and headed for the door. The same inquisitive intern walked briskly towards Shavon and relayed her information for the sorority tickets.

It was almost noon and Shavon had some time to relax before her 2 pm appointment with Pastor Dallas. Since she was only a hop, skip, and a jump away from the mall, she decided to run by and look at some of the formal gowns at Bloomingdales. Shavon didn't want to look like a prom queen for the ball, but she did want to look classy and sleek. With the colors for the ball being silver and royal blue, she hoped to find a silver gown. She envisioned it as being long, straight and very elegant. She wanted her appearance to be mysterious, yet eye-catching, and she figured she would also get an appointment with Elegance by Design to get her hair done. There was a stylist there named Sparkles who had some anointed hands.

Shavon knew that if she showed Sparkles the gown she was going to wear that she would be able to sculpture a masterpiece hairdo for the occasion. Shavon knew she had a defined body shape, but she had always been ashamed of showing her curves.

She thought her hips and buttocks drew too much unwanted attention when she had on clothes that clung to her.

Shavon was looking through the clearance rack when she heard her name being called clear across the store in a high-pitched voice. "Vonny! Vonny! Hey girl, it's me." Mo had on a pair of black dress slacks and a cream-colored halter top with a man's black blazer-style coat. As Mo got closer, Shavon could see that she was wearing a badge, which read: Sales Associate in Training. Shavon was glad that Mo had gotten a job and prayed that she would keep this one longer than her normal fourteen days.

With much confidence in her voice, "Vonny girl, if you find something, let me know 'cause I get a twenty percent discount. I'll hook you up."

Shavon just replied, "Okay, I'll let you know."

Mo stared at Shavon and said, "Oh, by the way, have you heard that Kenneth and that girlfriend of his are engaged?"

Shavon's heart tugged at her a little bit. Kenneth was getting married before her. Shavon swallowed all her hurt, smiled, and said, "No, but tell him God bless and tell her to read Psalm 71 daily."
Mo said, "Okay girl, I'll tell them. Bye."

Continuing her search through the dress racks, Shavon skimmed through the slim pickings more than twenty times before she found a dress that she knew she could not resist. It was perfect! She just knew it was the one. It was a black dress with spaghetti straps and a large rhinestone pendant in the midriff section – it was the pendant that caught her eye. Shavon held up the dress and admired it from all angles. She liked it but had really wanted something silver or gray. Shavon glanced at the size noting it was a size 9. She then looked at the price tag, not believing her eyes: it read $19.99! The original price was $169. Shavon was going to get this dress; it was perfect for the ball. In this dress she could see herself in the arms of Travis, swaying to some John Legend tune or maybe Kenny G; Shavon was such a daydreamer. She imagined herself dancing and prancing across the floor with Travis and him smiling at her as if she were the only woman in the room. She still believed in fairytales and didn't care who knew it. With the dress in her hand, she approached the checkout counter. She did not dare go to Mo's counter. She had enough of her for one day plus she didn't want to talk about Kenneth and his fiancée again.

The associate scanned the dress and said, "Sister, today is your lucky day! This dress has been marked down to $8.68 tax included." Shavon stood there in complete bewilderment. She had never really gotten anything that cheap in her whole life! Shavon had heard of Alana's shopping miracles but had never experienced one herself. Shavon gladly gave the associate $10 and whistled her way out of the store. She felt like God was really on her side today. She had twenty tentative ticket sales for the ball plus she had found a dress for way under $100. She felt blessed and highly favored.

Glancing at her watch, she saw that she had thirty-five minutes before she was to meet with Pastor Dallas so she drove through Starbucks and got an iced coffee mocha before heading towards the church. While driving, she said a little prayer. Shavon did not want the spirit of confusion to shadow her mission which was to talk to Pastor Dallas about the impact of having her car towed and the way it made her feel. Shavon didn't want this to happen again to her or another member and she surely did not want a visitor to go through the same ordeal. Shavon was unsure how Pastor Dallas would receive her, but she was going to stand up for what she felt was right.

As she approached the church, she saw several cars in the parking lot. She looked over at the space that had said 'Pastor's Parking Only' but the sign was no longer there. Shavon assumed they must have moved it closer to the administrative office for convenience. Shavon found a space between the Church Member of the Month spot and the handicapped parking. She checked herself in the mirror to make sure she looked appropriate and proceeded towards the church office door. She pressed the intercom button and was greeted by the same crude voice she had heard over the phone when she called for her appointment. Shavon kept her response to, "Good afternoon! I have a 2 o'clock appointment with Pastor Dallas."

She assumed it was the same receptionist who replied, "Sweetie, he's in a very important meeting.

You can wait or reschedule."

Shavon said, "I will just wait, please." And wait she did. She had not even been invited in out of the blistering heat. Shavon was getting heated herself, so she pressed the intercom button again and said, "Excuse me, but would it be possible to wait for Pastor Dallas in the lobby, please. The voice on the other side murmured something Shavon couldn't understand, but she finally caught, "I guess so; let me get up from here and come open the door."

Shavon couldn't wait to see who was on the other side. To Shavon's surprise, when the door finally swung open, after what seemed like several minutes, it was Sister Brown. Shavon felt mortified in her spirit. Sister Brown was First Lady Dallas' sister. Sister Brown was on every auxiliary and had served as president on more than one. Shavon had heard that Sister Brown ran a tighter ship than Sister Karen. Hard to believe, but Shavon had heard from other choir members, as well as those in the outreach ministry and church activity committee, that she did not even play the radio, she was so strict.

Shavon didn't know Sister Brown, but she always looked like something around her smelled. Some people thought she had suffered a stroke or something, the way she kept her lips all twisted up all the time. Sister Brown looked Shavon up and down in about four seconds flat. She pointed to a couch that was in a corner and grunted something Shavon did not think was a Bible verse!

Shavon wanted to call her job to let someone in the office know her whereabouts. Even though she had put it on the sign in/sign out board, she knew people never looked there. On the church's phone she found nearby, she called Maria, who answered on the first ring.

"Hi, Maria. How is Rico?"

"He's fine. I took him in for an appointment this morning and the doctor said he has an ear infection. Dr. Clifford gave him two prescriptions so he should be fine." Maria continued to say that she had come in so she could work on the public relations promotions for the Community Unity Ball and process the travel stipends for next week.

Shavon felt warm inside; once again, Maria had outdone herself. Shavon asked if she had any messages and Maria said, "No messages, but you did receive two dozen red roses about fifteen minutes ago."

Shavon was speechless. She thought about who they could possibly be from. "Maybe Clayson thanking me," she thought, "or even Kenneth trying to call a truce, since he was getting married." She even thought they could be from the board of directors as they had sent her flowers before. Maria asked Shavon if she would like her to read the card and since Shavon was so anxious about who they were from, she replied, "Yes." Maria read the card, "The card does not have a name, it just says, 'I am sorry, what about 9 pm tonight?'" Shavon instantly knew the flowers had come from Travis, and then she wondered how he knew where she worked. Since she had not told him, she became a little uneasy wondering if Travis was a stalker. To Maria, however, she said, "I've decided to take the afternoon off. Please place the roses in my office and I will see you tomorrow."

Shavon looked at her watch while hanging up the phone and noted it was 2:23 pm. She had been waiting to see Pastor Dallas for about 30 minutes. As Shavon was about to approach Sister Brown, the conference door opened and out walked Pastor Dallas, Deacon Smith, Deacon Ryles, and Elder White. Pastor Dallas greeted Shavon while the other three had looks of contention on their faces and said nothing. The men exited the door and disappeared. Within two minutes, Pastor Dallas reappeared and said, "Sister Washington, I am sorry for keeping you waiting. Please, follow me." Pastor Dallas was wearing a pair of jeans and a Sean John shirt. Shavon had never seen him 'dressed down' before. She followed him into his study. Shavon was feeling a bit edgy and even felt like just leaving, but she sat down and looked around the room. Pastor Dallas had degrees and all types of awards and certificates lining his walls. Shavon noticed a plaque from Edward Waters College. Shavon had a cousin who had also graduated from Edward Waters College in the early 90s who was now coaching basketball in Orlando.

Pastor Dallas was arranging some documents on his desk and very casually said, "Sister Washington, what is on your heart today?" He then apologized, "Sister Washington, it has been one heck of a day; please, let us pray." Pastor Dallas prayed and in Shavon's heart, she knew he was going through something himself as he seemed a bit broken. After prayer, Shavon really wanted to leave. He paused for a few seconds before saying "Amen."

Shavon could tell that Pastor Dallas was troubled within his spirit as he stood to his feet and paced the floor. He faced her and said, "Sister Washington, First Peter 5:8 says that the devil is busy and roaming the earth to see who he may destroy. You have to be careful who you let into your 'Christian camp'. Some people may not always be for you." Shavon didn't know where all this was going, but she just sat still and listened. Pastor Dallas went on, "How could I know the enemy was right up under my nose dotting all my I's and crossing all my T's? Lord, have mercy upon me. Sister Washington, I know why you are here and I am terribly sorry for the confusion you had to go through." Shavon was thinking to herself, how could he specifically know her situation? Pastor Dallas said, "Sister Washington, I did not have your car towed. I was unaware of a lot of things that were going on in this church. It wasn't until last week that the deacons brought some issues to my attention. The members have been talking and a few have even left the church. I have to make a major decision to pull the problem up from the root or leave the pulpit."

Shavon felt that Pastor Dallas needed a listening ear so she relaxed and sat back in her chair. Pastor Dallas, speaking with a noticeably heavy heart said, "I trusted the Lord's business to the hands of the enemy. I thought she was looking out for the church's best interest, but it was all about her and her own vain glory. She used control and hatred and now she has separated the church. She has a Jezebel spirit and used her authority to manipulate and gain control. The deacons have told me that either she goes or I go. I have to fire her from her paid administrative position and remove her from her positions within the church. She has done things in my name that I never approved of. She has had cars towed, been crude to members and business contacts on the phone. She has degraded members, lied, and caused havoc in the church and in my home. She must be reprimanded to save the remainder of The Word Baptist Church. The difficulty is that she is family." Pastor Dallas lowered his head and began to weep. He said, between sobs, "I feel so humiliated that I fell into her trap. I have to publicly apologize to the congregation for being weak." Shavon wondered what he meant by weak.

He said, "Sister Washington, it is not the church I'm worried about, it is my wife. How will she ever forgive me for lying with her sister? I have betrayed my wife and I am so very sorry. I have allowed my flesh to direct my path and not the Lord. I have sinned and fallen short of His glory." Shavon wanted to throw up as she, too, felt weak. Pastor Dallas could tell that he had said too much, but he continued quickly, "The deacons are giving me until 5 pm and I have not even spoken with my wife about this yet. Temptation is a stinger."

Shavon couldn't find anything to say. She prayed quickly to herself, and then said, "Pastor, you need some serious counsel. I think you need to pray until you get a word from God and then go home and talk with your wife. Pastor, there is nothing, nothing too hard for God to handle. First Lady Dallas loves you and she will forgive you. Do the right thing, Pastor, and God will reward you."

"Sister Washington, please forgive me. I pray you will not be discouraged by the actions of the church again."

At that moment, Shavon saw another side to her pastor. He was a man, a caring and compassionate man, who had to deal with real life issues; and now he was going to have to practice what he preached. He was going to have to wait on the Lord.

Shavon knew that being a pastor was a hard job, but today gave her insight into its difficulties first hand. As Shavon was about to grab her purse and leave, Pastor Dallas said, "Sister Washington, once again, thank you for letting me unload all my problems on you today. Please do not share this information with anyone, but pray for my strength and direction through this trial." The phone rang and startled them both. Pastor Dallas answered the phone and he had a disgusted look on his face and said, "Yes,

Sister Brown. By the way, I need to talk to you as soon as this meeting is over".

Shavon felt that Pastor Dallas was ready for spiritual warfare. As Shavon left the church, all she could say was "Amen! Let the preacher say Amen."

That evening at 9:00, Shavon logged onto her computer. She noticed that Travis was there, in his idle mode and had been since around 8:44 pm, waiting for her. Shavon felt slightly uncomfortable. She had not talked with Travis in what seemed like years, even though it had been just this morning. The first thing Shavon wrote was, "Thanks for the roses today! I have not seen them myself yet, but I heard they were strikingly gorgeous."

Travis wrote back, "I had to do something to get myself back in good standing with you."

Shavon thought that was quite cute and wrote, "So tell me, what has been going on in My Black Emperor's life lately?"

"Work and more work, in addition to helping my friends with their issue." Continuing on, he also wrote, "I have been trying to be a supportive friend."

Shavon thought this friend has to be a good friend because he is investing a lot of time into their relationship, not to mention standing her up on their previously planned phone date. Since she did not want to spend all their time talking about his friends, whoever they might be, she changed the subject and filled Travis in on all the adventures she had gone through over the last couple of weeks. She told him about Clayson and Emerald, the meeting with her pastor, and her plans for the Community Unity Ball.

Shavon was feeling good that she finally had someone to talk with. She really missed talking with Alana and was feeling like things between her and Alana were becoming distant. She was going to have to find a way to stop her best friend from putting in so many hours at work. She was missing her terribly. Shavon thought about telling Travis how much she had missed him and that she was not going to cut any corners, but instead she wrote, "I have missed talking with you."

Without hesitation on his part, Travis responded by saying,"I really missed you too and can't wait until I see your beautiful smile." When Shavon read his reply, she felt mushy on the inside. Shavon was falling in love with Travis and she was also trying to avoid her heart being hurt, so she mentally slammed on the emotional brakes and again thought of something else and questioned Travis by writing, "How did you know where to send the flowers?"

Travis wrote that he had spent half a day calling and researching the Internet. He wrote her, "I remembered you saying you worked for a non-profit organization, so I searched every organization online until I found you." He further confessed that once he found her organization, he just about had to pull teeth to get confirmation that she worked there so he could have the flowers delivered. He ended his writing by stating, "Your administrative assistant runs a tight ship."

Travis was so impressive in that he was saying and doing all the right things. She had to be so careful and make sure this was in the Lord's will before she fell even more in love with Travis than she already was.

Shavon knew she was going to have to really pray about this issue, lying prostrate on the floor before God. She did not want to find herself in the same situation she had been with Kenneth. Shavon had made some really stupid mistakes because she did not consult God like she should have in her relationship with Kenneth. He had taken her through hell and back with a stick of dynamite in her own hand and Shavon didn't want to experience that ever again.

The computer beeped, and she read, "I cannot wait to be in your arms, Shavon." She smiled intensely; she had been thinking almost that very thought but had not wanted to say it first. She really had good vibes about Travis; she was just still on the leery side. She wished that she was bold enough to meet him in person. As they had been chatting for three hours by now, Shavon was sleepy; she knew that she was going to have to say goodbye first so she wrote, "Goodbye, Travis."

He responded, "Goodnight, Shavon, I care a lot about you and I will talk with you tomorrow. How about the same place, different time? I have some things to do tomorrow but would 10 pm be too late for you?" "No, that is fine. Anytime."

They logged off; and while Shavon had the thought of questioning what it was that Travis had to do tomorrow, she changed her mind, determining that she was not going to worry about the issue but was just going to enjoy the moment.

She fell to her knees and prayed. Shavon was going to have straight talk with her heavenly father tonight. She was falling for Travis and, while it was exhilarating, it also scared her. Shavon prayed for God to reveal if Travis was the one for her. She wanted to know if he was to be her "husband". Shavon said, "Lord I have feelings for him and even contemplate asking him to come over. Father, I know you said in Proverbs 4:23 to guard my heart, for it is the wellspring of life. I'm trying, but I also think I am falling in love. Father, in the past I put my trust in a man and he let me down. I don't want to travel that same road again. Lord, please help me so that I do not act out of impulse but follow where You lead me. Lord I can't lie. I have been lusting in my body for Travis and I ask that You take that feeling away. Lord, cool me down. I need help."

Shavon couldn't believe she was talking to God like this, but at the same time, she realized she needed to be real with herself and with God – He already knew her thoughts and her heart anyway. Even though she had never seen Travis, she felt like she was in love; but for all she knew, he could be some really unattractive maniac.

On the other side, Travis was also really starting to care a lot for Shavon. He had never really let a woman keep his attention the way she did. He wanted to be in her life forever. He, too, went down on his knees and prayed, "Lord, Shavon is so different from other women who have been in my life. You know her Lord. You made her to be gentle and kind Lord, she is the woman I need in my life. I'm falling in love with her. I would love to have her as my wife for life. Lord, in Proverbs 18:22, You said that he who finds a wife finds a good thing and Lord, I think I have found her. Lord, I want to invite her over, but I am so afraid of my flesh, for it is weak. Lord, I know she is a phenomenal woman because she was made in Your image. Please give me a sign if it's Your will for her to become my wife. Amen."

Shavon and Travis had connected in the spirit. They were chatting every day and sometimes three to four times a day over the phone. The conversations were getting more and more intense in nature. Shavon was becoming anxious as she wanted to have a face-to-face with Travis, but God hadn't given her the sign yet and she was not going to be disobedient to the Holy Spirit. Shavon had to admit that she was falling deep for Travis; and while God knew the same when it came to Travis, Shavon did not yet know that – well, not really.

A few days later, Shavon finally cornered Alana and told her about Travis. Alana told her that she would support her. Alana said she would have him investigated to see what his story was, but Shavon told her "no, thank you." Alana remembered that Shavon had prayed plenty of nights when they were roommates for an ambitious, Christian man, who shared the same interests and desires that she had. Shavon knew that there was something special about Travis, and she intended to stick around and find out what it was. He made her smile whenever they had time to chat online.

She felt like he could be the one God intended for her, yet she still had butterflies in her stomach and was not sure she could trust herself. But she did trust in the Lord, so she was going to wait.

Whoso findeth a wife findeth a good thing,
and obtaineth favour of the LORD.
Proverbs 18:22

Shavon, I have been contemplating about asking you to be my significant other. I have been thinking about you a lot lately and I realize that you are a wonderful person. I would love to get to know you better." Shavon was thunderstruck. She tried to talk, but it seemed as if her voice box had been shut down and her hands were shaking uncontrollably...

CHAPTER X

UNITED WE STAND

The weeks had just rushed by so fast. Shavon still had her final meeting with the board of directors for review of all the expenses and to discuss last minute formalities. To date, ticket sales for the ball were well over twenty-two thousand dollars and that didn't account for the RSVPs that indicated that they would pay at the door. Maria, Diane, and other supporting staff had done a magnificent job of organizing the ticket sales and marketing the event.

Diane had returned to work two weeks ago; looking rested and rejuvenated. She looked like the old Diane and Shavon was happy to know things were working out for her and her family. Diane had shared with Shavon that her marriage was in the repairing stage and her husband had just completed a six-week in–patient substance abuse program. He was doing well and had already returned to work part-time, spending more time with Eden. Diane also expressed she just had to thank God every day for his deliverance and for such supportive friends who had stood by them through these trying times.

Shavon had confirmed with Clayson and his agent that he would be in attendance at the ball. Shavon had asked Clayson and Emerald to stay at her home, but he insisted they would get a suite at the Ritz Carlton since his agent had already booked their rooms. Clayson said Emerald was being a true celebrity because she loved hanging out in the spas and having lunch poolside. Clayson's agent had arranged for him and Emerald to visit two elementary schools on the southeast side of town on Thursday and Friday since they were already going to be in town for the ball.

One of the principals was an African American woman and she had really worked hard to turn the school around. She had a Lazarus experience of taking the school from an "F" status to an "A" status and the community was really rallying around her, especially one of the local churches. The pastor of that church had made it his personal mission to visit the school several times a month to mentor the children. The local news was already featuring Clayson's arrival and had even thrown in a plug for the ball.

Shavon had planned on taking Clayson and Emerald to dinner on Thursday night. Shavon asked

Clayson if he wanted a formal dinner, but he candidly told her no. He was tired of all that type of atmosphere and he just wanted to have a night off. Shavon knew Clayson loved visiting sport bars, so she decided to take him to the Gators Nest Restaurant near the campus. Shavon knew Clayson would just love the scene and the food was to-die-for.

Alana and Drayton were supposed to join them. Shavon was hoping that Alana didn't cancel. Shavon still hadn't found the time to talk with her about her excessive work schedule. Shavon knew all work and no play could be hazardous to her mental health and her relationships. Shavon missed hanging out together; to Shavon, it seemed like it had been forever. A part of Shavon wished that she had a relationship as united as Alana's and Drayton's because when they were together, they seemed like a fitted puzzle piece. Drayton showered Alana with love and attention. He treated her as if she was a rare jewel. He just loved her so much. Shavon couldn't figure out why they weren't married, but it wasn't her business.

Shavon missed the male companionship in her life as she had not been in a relationship since Kenneth. Even though her relationship with him had been toxic, she sometimes enjoyed him just being around, when he was around. Shavon thought it was insane for her to just want someone around without any commitment or longevity in the plan. She never again wanted to experience that type of loneliness again, but she still had to wait for the lord to send her a husband because she knew she could not take any foolishness from another man ever again.

Shavon wasn't going to compromise her faith in God. She was going to wait until He sent someone into her life to be her lifetime partner and not her bedtime buddy. There was a difference, a BIG difference. Shavon had a brief moment of sadness as she pondered on the upcoming ball. She felt proud that she had helped coordinate such a beneficial event. She was joyful in her soul that the participants in her program would benefit from the monetary contributions and the possibility that someone would be forever changed. She was even more blessed to have had the support of her family and friends to help her celebrate this great occasion, yet there was that certain something that was still missing.

Shavon's parents would be in attendance and she was so happy they were coming. She knew they wouldn't miss it for the world. She was expecting them on Friday around noon. Shavon's mother was so proud of both her children. She had been bragging at her women's ministry meeting and Sister Parker had mentioned it to her daughter, Ericka, who attended high school with Shavon. Ericka then posted the event on the high school alumni's website and Shavon had been getting congratulations from classmates online around the world, some she didn't even remember knowing.

Shavon had mailed Alana and Drayton two complimentary tickets for the Community Unity Ball, but Alana had already purchased two tickets online so she asked Shavon to give them to a couple who would appreciate it. Shavon had just the couple in mind, Mr. Clyde and his wife. Shavon previously spoken with Mr. Clyde and he was almost in tears with joy. He had taken the tickets home to his wife and asked her if she wanted to attend. Mr. Clyde said she was so excited she had called all her home mission friends and told them about it. She was happy and was looking forward to coming. Mr. Clyde said they hadn't been out to a formal event since his niece had gotten married nine years previously.

Shavon knew Alana was getting herself together because she lived for outings like this. Alana loved dressing up and this would give her an excuse to shop. Shavon had to still shop for her accessories. She had decided to wear the gown she had purchased at Bloomingdales. She had tried on the dress numerous times and loved it more and more. Alana had suggested that Shavon look for accessories at Adonis Attractions. It was a very classy boutique, owned by a young woman who had majored in fashion design and now was an entrepreneur. Alana said she had the best accessories in town.

Shavon wanted to find a rhinestone choker necklace to accent her dress. She had already found an elegant sandal heel-type shoe with a rhinestone broach centered in the middle of the shoe that she thought would be perfect. She found it at TJ MAXX for less than fifty dollars. Shavon was going to be glamorous and all for under $100. All she could say was, "You go girl!"

Shavon had scheduled her hair appointment with Elegance by Design. She was to meet with Sparkles to decide which style she felt would help define the look she wanted to go with her dress. Shavon had decided herself that she was comfortable with a silk wrap, but she would be fine with a very cute up-do, as well. She was going to let the professional create something unique for her.

The excitement of the whole evening was starting to hover over her life like a black cloud over a baseball game on a sunny day; she was beginning to get a little jumpy. She said a silent prayer and asked God for patience and a sense of peace. Shavon felt that everything was going to be alright, she had faith; it was as if she was planning a wedding and was now having wedding jitters. Shavon thought about the serenity prayer and it brought her peace by reciting. Peace in knowing that God would give her the strength to accept the things she could not change and the wisdom to know the difference.

Shavon had checked and double checked every item from the caterers to the band and everything seemed to be going as planned. She had always been concerned about other people and wanted to make sure that Maria was prepared for the ball so she walked out to her desk. Maria was sitting there with a gigantic smile on her face. It was Maria's personality that kept things going around the work place. She was one of those people who were so warm and inviting.

"So, what are your plans for the ball, Maria?" Shavon asked.

"I'm so excited! I have purchased a gown and my hubby is going to rent a tux." Maria replied adding, "My mother-in-law is going to watch the children for us for the whole weekend!" Maria smiled and continued, "Friday starts our weekend." One would think she was describing the weekend away as if it were a honeymoon she never had or a prom she never attended all wrapped into one. Maria had gotten so excited, she converted to Spanish, "Voy a tener un fin de semana caliente que chisporrotea" (I'm going to have a sizzling hot weekend). Shavon was so happy for her.

Maria then asked Shavon what her plans for her family were. Shavon said, "Clayson and Emerald will be in town on Thursday and we are going to meet for dinner. My parents are then coming in on Friday around noon."

Maria wanted to ask Shavon if she had a date for Saturday night, but felt so self-conscious about asking so she didn't. Maria's husband had an older friend, Angel, who was a widower. Maria was thinking of hooking Shavon up with him. Angel's wife, Marbella, had died in a fatal car crash three years ago. He was a respectable guy, owned his own mechanic shop in town, and was raising his daughter, Mariabelle. Maria knew that dating was a sensitive subject for Shavon and she did not want to put a damper on her weekend.

As Shavon was driving home from work, her mind, as usual, began to wander. She wondered what Travis was doing. Shavon couldn't deny the fact that she wished Travis could accompany her to the ball. Shavon was going to casually mention it again tonight and see if he might be available.

The house was silent as usual when Shavon got home. Later in the evening, she was lying across her bed reading a book written by Tia Wilson, when the phone rang. She reached for the phone to see who was calling and it was Travis. She wasn't expecting him to call. She thought they were going to chat online. As she didn't want to appear desperate, she let the phone ring a few more times before answering.

"Hello?" she answered.

"Hello!" There was exhilaration in his voice. He seemed to be happy about something and Shavon was going to try to find out what this was all about. She was hoping his plans had been canceled and that he was going to be available to accompany her to the ball. "I have been waiting all day just to hear your voice." Travis explained, "So how are you?"

"I am doing fine. I have just been reading a book from a local author and it is pretty good. I am going to purchase several copies and give them out for presents at Christmas." Shavon was so happy that Travis had called and said that he was thinking about her. Travis was so sweet. "So, Travis, I was wondering if your plans had changed for Saturday night and if so, if you were available?"

Travis was silent for a few minutes before responding, "I'm sorry, Shavon, but I had promised my friend and his wife that I would go to dinner with them. They asked me months ago. I am terribly sorry, Shavon."

Shavon had to admit to herself that she was disappointed. Her heart was aching as she had hoped he would have said he was available.

"Would a late night movie be okay?" he asked.

Shavon liked the idea but declined the offer because her parents would be in town and she didn't want to skip out on them, so she asked for a rain check. Travis apologized again for not being available. He sounded so sincere, so she just let the matter drop.

Shavon's phone beeped so she asked Travis if he would hold. She clicked over and it was Alana. She sounded like she was out of breath. She asked Shavon what was up. "I was here walking on this treadmill and thought I would call and ask you if you had a date for the ball on Saturday."

"No," Shavon replied. "I am going to pass this year. Let me call you back; I am on the phone with Travis and I do not want to keep him waiting." Alana said, "Well, if you change your mind let me know."

"Okay. I love you. Bye." Shavon clicked back over to Travis who was sitting there patiently.

"So, you are back. Who was that? Your other cyber man?" he asked jokingly.

Shavon laughed and saucily replied, "No. One cyber man is more than I can handle at this time."

"You know, your voice is beautiful, Shavon." It was easy for Shavon to be flattered with her feelings for Travis being what they were. "Your voice is comforting, Travis."

Travis had never felt this way about another woman since his last relationship had ended when his college sweetheart, Shyanne, had left him for his fraternity brother, Jeffrey Love-Bandit Middleton. Travis had been left wounded and had just decided to never love again. "Shavon, I have been contemplating about asking you to be my significant other. I have been thinking about you a lot lately and I realize that you are a wonderful person. I would love to get to know you better."

Shavon was thunderstruck. She tried to talk, but it seemed as if her voice box had been shut down and her hands were shaking uncontrollably. "Travis, please do not say things you do not mean. I had a bad experience in my last relationship and I am still in the healing process. At the same time, I am interested in you so I would like to continue moving forward slowly."

Travis was in agreement as he too had been hurt and responded, "I agree. I have been hurt as well and had it not been for prayer and supportive friends, I would have been in a psycho ward."

Shavon could relate to his hurt. A part of her wanted to know his story, but she also knew now wasn't the appropriate time.

Travis was happy he had been able to give her an indication of how serious he was about her. He had not been on a date in what seemed like an eternity. Travis needed someone in his life to share his visions, aspirations, and dreams. Lately, Travis had moments of such loneliness; especially since he lived in town alone while his family resided in Mississippi. He did work and attend church and sometimes socialized with a few friends he had met and their families, but the longing remained for a family of his own. Travis was ready to marry and have children and lots of them.

Shavon had the same issue with loneliness. She could not even remember the last time she had been out for a night of fun which was one reason why she was looking forward to the ball. The one thing that bothered her was that she would not be going with Travis.

Time had slipped away from them, but Shavon could feel her body tugging at her to get some rest. "I better let you go so you can be well rested for tomorrow." She said.

"I was thinking the same thing, but I didn't want to go." Shavon understood; she had been enjoying their conversation, which was a lot different than hiding behind a keyboard. Before he let her go, Travis said, "I have to tell you something."

Shavon braced herself as she had no idea what Travis might tell her. She was not prepared for him to tell her he was a convicted felon or something else equally bizarre. "Okay, what is it?" She asked.

Travis just let the words trickle from his lips, "Shavon Washington, I think I am falling in love with you. I find it very hard to say goodnight and I think about you all through the day."

"Ditto" was all Shavon could muster. She was in such shock.

Shavon was the first to hang up, but she continued to stare at the phone receiver. She finally said a little prayer and then went to bed to sleep.

Travis had made a bold statement tonight and he had to tell God about it. "Lord," he prayed, "Thank you for the opportunity to talk with Shavon. Lord, if you see fit, I would love to see her in person. Lord, please tell me if she is the wife You have ordained for me. I could really use a sign. Amen."

Thursday night had finally arrived. Shavon was waiting outside the restaurant waiting for her 'celebrity brother' and his daughter. It was a pleasant night to be outdoors. Shavon was so excited about seeing them again that she was twenty minutes early. She had talked earlier with Clayson and they had agreed to meet at 8 pm. Shavon had stopped at Target and bought Emerald a nice pink and canary-colored bathing suit and matching pool slippers along with a sun visor. Shavon knew how prissy Emerald was, so she added a pair of shades to complete the outfit. Shavon placed all the items in a sunflower canvas bag for easy carrying to the beach. She really hoped Emerald would love it, although she was pretty sure she would.

Shavon was so very pleased to have this time with Clayson and Emerald. She could not remember the last time they had gotten together. She had great admiration for Clayson. Clayson had been Shavon's hero when they were growing up. Shavon loved her older brother. During the challenging times Clayson had, Shavon prayed for him everyday. She always prayed for emotional wellbeing and the reunification of his family. Shavon had seen God move in a mighty way and she was so very thankful.

Shavon was reapplying her lip gloss when she heard a faint voice squeal, "Auntie Vonny!" Shavon looked up and it was Emerald running towards her. She was wearing a cute Baby Phat jean outfit with a pair of silver sandals and a silver handbag. Shavon read the joy on Emerald's face and opened her arms to engulf Emerald and give her a kiss on her rosy cheeks. Shavon put Emerald down and gave her the gift she had bought for her. While Emerald was investigating the contents of the bag, Clayson walked up and his face was glowing. Clayson looked like he had before times had gotten so hard for him. Clayson was a handsome man; he was tall with caramel skin and his features were very classy. As usual, Clayson was well groomed. Clayson hugged her like he was trying to say, "Thank you."Shavon allowed him to hug her until he wanted to let go. When he let go, he reached down and gave her a box. Inside was a picture that had been taken when they were children one Halloween. Clayson was dressed, of course, as a football player and Shavon had dressed like a princess. Shavon was tickled he had put so much thought into a gift that would stir her soul, especially since she was not even expecting anything except the joy of his company.

They went inside the restaurant and Clayson was immediately recognized by the waiter who escorted them to a table. Clayson didn't seem to let his celebrity status affect him, remaining a humble and down to earth type person. Clayson let his eyes wander while they walked back to their table and Shavon and Emerald were seated. He saw the walls filled with Gator greats from all different sports. There was Ricky Nattiel, Eric Rhett, Emmitt Smith, Willie Jackson, and, Mareese Speights, and more. Once Shavon and Emerald were seated, Clayson took his seat having been raised to be a gentleman.

Shavon asked about their trip and Clayson said they had flown in from Dallas where he and Emerald had just finished a photo shoot for a sporting goods company. He told her it had been hot in Texas and he was glad to be somewhere where the heat was more tolerable. Clayson said he believed that Emerald had turned a shade darker in those three days in Texas. Clayson went on to tell her that while he was out there he had wanted to visit T. D. Jakes' church, The Potters House. He mentioned that he frequently received prayer from his ministry when he had been going through all his issues and as a result, he sowed into the ministry every month. He wanted to meet T. D. Jakes in person to say thanks. Clayson was indeed a miracle.

When God called him forth, he rose and came out of his depression and decided to live life to the fullest.

Shavon was enjoying spending time with her big brother and her niece. The waitress came over to the table and Clayson ordered a chicken finger basket for Emerald as it was her favorite. He then ordered a twenty-piece turbo hot chicken wing platter for himself. Shavon ordered a Caesar salad with a side order of mild wings.

Shavon's cell phone rang. She glanced at the caller ID and noticed it was Alana so she answered. Alana had to cancel as she could not get away from the store and Drayton was still in traffic trying to make it to Gainesville from Jacksonville. Alana wanted to let Shavon know she just didn't want to skip out on her. Shavon was disappointed but she was enjoying having Clayson and Emerald to herself. Before the food arrived, Clayson had diverted his attention to the wide screen television located on the wall in front of him. A Gator basketball game was playing and a few of the players were being interviewed.

Shavon started a conversation with Emerald who had been sitting quietly writing in a small journal type book. She seemed quite focused. Shavon asked her what she was doing. Emerald said she was keeping a journal of all the places that she and her daddy had visited so she could share it with her mama when she called. Shavon thought that was probably quite therapeutic for Emerald. No one had really discussed Jasmine since they had left Washington, at least not to Shavon.

The food arrived and they all began to eat. Emerald ate almost all of her food; Clayson said she was a picky eater like Jasmine. Clayson also mentioned that Emerald was so much like Jasmine it petrified him sometimes. While Clayson was talking about Jasmine, there was sadness in his eyes. Shavon believed that Clayson still loved Jasmine in his own way. Shavon asked if Emerald had been to visit Jasmine. Clayson told her that their father had taken her about three weeks prior. He said it had been a bitter sweet moment for the two of them. Clayson continued that Dad had told him he cried all the way back home.

"Jasmine calls Emerald every Sunday no matter where we are and writes at least two times a week if not three." Clayson said that if the letters arrive and they are not in town their mother would Fed-Ex them to Emerald.

Clayson cleared his throat and said, "Jasmine even wrote me a letter once about two months ago, but I have yet to open it." Clayson continued, "One day I will when God says it's time."

Shavon just reached over and squeezed Clayson's hand. Emerald could see Clayson was struggling so she hopped up in his lap and gave him a peak on the cheek and hugged him. Having Emerald around was all Clayson needed in his life and he was so very thankful.

Clayson glanced at his watch. Time had flown! "It is getting late and my little princess has to get her beauty rest."

Emerald sat there smiling and said, "Thank you Auntie Vonny. I love my gifts. I will wear it tomorrow."

The waitress and an older gentleman approached the table. The gentleman said, "Mr. Washington thank you and your family for dining with us tonight. On behalf of the owner, we would like to pay for your dinner if you would please allow it."

"Thank you, that is very kind," Clayson said.

Shavon nudged Clayson and teased him, "I am going to have to hang out with you more often if you get this kind of treatment." The waitress grinned at her and shyly asked Clayson if she could have a picture of him and his family. Clayson glanced at Shavon and she nodded her head in approval. Emerald loved taking pictures so she smiled and the waitress brought a camera out of her apron and snapped a few shots.

Shavon really enjoyed her night out with her family. She would remember this night for the rest of her life.

As Shavon headed home she thought of Travis and how he would have loved to have had dinner with Clayson, Emerald, and her. She knew another opportunity would show itself and he would be there, of that she was sure. Shavon knew that Travis was a fan of Clayson from his football days.

It was two days before the Community Unity Ball and Shavon was overcome with emotion. She had made a good first impression with the board and now she was going to have to WOW the guests.

Shavon looked Travis straight in the eyes and then closed her eyes and laid her head on his shoulder. With great relief, she sighed, "I believe the wait is over." The band had long stopped playing, but Travis and Shavon didn't realize it because they were in their own little world...

CHAPTER XI

SATURDAY NIGHT AT THE COMMUNITY UNITY BALL

Shavon had to say so herself: she was looking quite elegant! The dress was indeed a show stopper. Everything was in place – her hair and makeup; she looked like a celebrity, she looked tremendous. Shavon arrived early. She wanted to make sure that everything was going as planned. The food looked and smelled scrumptious, the band was setting up in their designated area, the stage had been set, and the decorations looked perfect for the setting. Shavon couldn't ask for a better coming together of it all.

As Shavon observed all the preparations taking place, she paused for a few minutes: "Thank you, Lord. You have done such a wonderful job." She did not want to cry and ruin her makeup, but she felt tears begin to well up in her eyes so she tried hard to relax.

The crowd began to filter in. Shavon gracefully walked through the mass and spoke to her guests and some of the participants and their families. Shavon spotted Maria and her husband. They looked like a high school prom king and queen; they looked good together. Shavon got close enough to her and said, "You look awesome! So how has your evening been without the children?"

"It has been fabulous!" Maria said with a huge grin on her face.

Shavon tried to enjoy herself, but she still felt empty without a date. The last company event, she had come with Kenneth. He spent more time around the food table than socializing and mingling with her. Shavon had made an oath that she would never bring him to a company event again because she had been so embarrassed.

Shavon noticed her parents entering the building. She had left them at her house to get dressed. Shavon's dad was wearing a black tux and her mom, an elegant green dress with silver accessories. Shavon had to admit, she had good-looking parents. She escorted them to the VIP table where they would be sitting. Shavon felt blessed to be surrounded by family and friends. As they approached the table, she heard a familiar voice calling, "Grandma! Grandaddy" It was Emerald. She looked very pretty in her lilac-colored dress with a cream shawl. Her hair was down and very curly. Emerald mentioned that her daddy was behind the stage with Mr. Thaddeus and asked her to have a seat with Auntie Vonny. Shavon's heart was about to leap out of her chest she was so full of joy. Once she had her parents seated, she continued to mingle and make sure everyone was doing okay. She thanked God she was wearing comfortable shoes; she was getting frequent walking miles going to and fro. Everyone looked great and the smiles on everyone's faces implied that they were having a good time.

Alana and Drayton finally arrived and Alana looked absolutely breath-taking, as always. There was no hair out of place or a smudge of makeup smeared. Alana looked like she had just stepped off a red carpet runway. Alana could've easily been mistaken for Vivica Fox. Drayton held Alana as if she was the Queen of Sheba; he was so proud to have her on his arm. Shavon chatted briefly with Alana and told her and Drayton to make their way to the VIP table where her parents and Emerald were sitting. Alana whispered in Shavon's ear, "Girl, you look so good you might just find you a husband tonight!"

Shavon just looked at her. "I wish."

As the night progressed everything continued to go as planned. Shavon saw Dr. Carrington, the head of the board. He was impressed with the way things had turned out thus far.

Clayson spoke elegantly; he had become a poised speaker. He spoke about the fitness campaign and his vision for helping children stay physically, emotionally, and spiritually fit. Clayson thanked the board for this opportunity to speak and thanked his parents and Shavon for the incredible support he had received from them. He then asked his agent to help him with a special presentation. Clayson's agent brought out a life-sized check in the amount of $20,000 to help support at-risk youth in the area. He received a standing ovation. Shavon was in awe; she had no idea he was going to do anything like this. She knew he was generous, but all she could say was "Thank you, Lord."

Shavon was to give the closing remarks, but she was too overcome with joy to say anything but "Thank you, thank you all; and especially, thank You, God." The event was nearing its end with only about an hour left in the night. Shavon was tired and all she could think about was climbing into her bed and going to sleep. She thought it was just plain courtesy for her to stay until the end to thank her guests so she made another round.

She saw Mr. Clyde and his wife, they looked so cute together. He just gave her the thumbs up sign and asked if they needed any help cleaning up. She told him no because they had it all covered and he should just enjoy the evening.

To Shavon's surprise, she saw Mo and some man sitting in the far corner. Mo was looking very sophisticated – there was nothing ghetto about her tonight. Mo gave Shavon a wink and mouthed, "I wouldn't have missed this for the world, and I love you."

Shavon was about to walk back to the table where her parents were sitting when she saw Diane out of the corner of her eye. She hardly recognized her. Diane looked ten years younger. She was wearing a cream-colored gown with gold accessories. She looked so alive, so refreshed. Shavon let out a gasp and said, "Diane, you look beautiful!"

Diane replied, "Boss, you look Bossy tonight." she said with a grin. "No, seriously, you look stunning."

Diane was sitting at the table with two handsome men. Shavon could tell one was her husband because of the pictures on her desk and she could see that her son, Eden, resembled him. She wasn't quite sure who the other gentleman was. Diane said, "Let me introduce you to my husband, Phillip. Phillip stood up and extended his hand and said, "Thank you for allowing my wife to have some time off; it was needed and appreciated."

Phillip then extended his hand and said, "May I introduce you to my friend, Mr. Travis Elliot."

Shavon froze like a deer in headlights. She had to quickly ask herself if Phillip just said Travis Elliott? Travis licked his lips and all Shavon saw was straight, white teeth. Travis extended his hand and said, "What a blessing it is to meet you, Shavon Washington. I am so very 'Grateful' to have met you tonight."

Diane and Phillip just looked at the two of them, trying to figure out if they understood what was happening. Shavon and Travis just stood gazing into each other's eyes not saying a word. Their spirits had just collided and it was wonderful.

Diane said, "Hello? Do you know each other?" "Yes," Travis said with a wide smile on his face. Shavon herself was still in shock. She couldn't stop staring at him. He had beautiful hazel brown eyes and pearly white teeth. He was as fine as she imagined him to be. Shavon knew she was probably looking confused with a blank look on her face so she finally shyly asked Travis if he wanted to dance.

Travis grabbed her by the hand and led her to the dance floor. The band was playing "My Funny Valentine" by Miles Davis. Shavon looked Travis straight in the eyes and then closed her eyes and laid her head on his shoulder. With great relief, she sighed, "I believe the wait is over." The band had long stopped playing, but Travis and Shavon didn't realize it because they were in their own little world. Everyone stood to their feet and applauded them. Shavon nervously took Travis by the hand and led him outside. She looked at him and asked, "Travis, did you know you would see me here tonight?"

No, but once I got here I realized that the dinner Diane and Phillip had invited me to was the ball. I have been watching you all night. When Clayson made his appearance, I knew I was in the right place. I was going to wait until the end of the night to approach you, but God wouldn't let me wait and you found me first."

Travis leaned over and planted a kiss on her cheek; Shavon almost melted. She responded, "I have to get back in or I know people will come out here looking for me. Please come with me to meet my parents?"

Travis grabbed her hand and let her lead the way.

Shavon was ecstatic. Since the day Travis had proposed, she had been on cloud nine. She felt complete; not because she had a man in her life, but because God had fulfilled his promise. The proposal had been somewhat unexpected even though she knew they were in love...

CHAPTER XII

A MATCH MADE IN HEAVEN

Six months later, Shavon didn't know what was involved with planning a wedding. She had thought planning the ball was a lot of work; she was now planning the most important day of her life. She had all the particulars worked out, but now it was time to make it all happen.

Shavon had always dreamed of a fairytale wedding. She wanted the long white wedding dress and a horse and carriage ride to take her to the church. She had seen these elaborate weddings on television and in wedding books, but realized she really was not into it that much anymore. She just wanted a small intimate wedding with family and close friends. Shavon's father told her anything she wanted to just let him know, he was going to pay for the whole wedding. She was his princess and he wanted it to be exactly what she hoped this special day would be. Shavon and Travis planned for a Valentine's Day wedding.

Choosing colors, she finally decided on crimson and white with a hint of silver. Shavon had asked Alana to be her maid of honor and Travis asked Phillip to be his best man. Emerald was going to be their flower princess and Eden was going to stand as the ring bearer. Shavon asked Pastor Dallas to officiate. Her father was going to escort her to her groom and he was very honored. All of Travis' family planned to make the trip too, as they were in Mississippi; this made Travis very happy. Travis' mother had never been to Florida and it seemed the only question she had for him was how far the wedding was going to be from Disney World. Travis' older sister, Belinda, was so happy for him that she cried when he told her that he had found his wife. Brenda had been praying for Travis to find a wife for years, especially since she had decided she was ready for nieces and nephews!

Maria and Diane were ecstatic. Diane had no clue that Travis was talking about Shavon when he would talk about his 'new friend'. Diane had thought several times to try and play cupid with the two of them, but she was too consumed with her own issues at the time. It came as a complete surprise the night of the ball when Diane discovered that they already knew one another. Diane felt it had to be a divine appointment from God.

When Travis was introduced to the Washington family, he was worried. He knew from the way Shavon talked about her father that he loved his daughter and he was going to be critiquing him from every angle to see if he was worthy of his baby girl. Travis knew he wouldn't have a problem building a rapport with Clayson because he felt like he already knew him and they had a lot in common, especially with football being a big focus for them both. Tarik, he thought, would just be a cordial person who would observe and feel him out along the way. He thought Shavon's mother was going to be the one with all the questions and Travis was prepared. He had lived in a house with his mother and sisters, so he knew all the right things to say. Shavon was overjoyed that everyone seemed to love Travis!"

On the day of the wedding, Travis was more nervous than a small town minister about to preach his trial sermon on his first Sunday in the pulpit. Travis was sweating so profusely that his best man Phillip had to manually cool him down using a church fan. Travis paced the floor, walking from the bathroom to the hall entrance. Travis couldn't believe that God had sent his angel. Travis had fervently prayed for the last two years for God to send someone who would love him just for him with no strings attached. Travis remembered asking God specifically for his soul mate, someone he could confide in and someone who loved the Lord. The Lord had told Travis He would give him a wife that would bring him much happiness and bliss. Today he would marry the woman God had chosen for him – his friend and lover. Travis had no idea when he joined that Christian online dating service he would actually find his wife. He had just been seeking for some companionship and something to ease his loneliness. He had been amazed when he found the woman he wanted to love and cherish for the rest of his life. Travis couldn't stop thanking God for his lifetime blessing. Travis thought about how he had thought Shavon was special from the first night they chatted. Even though he hadn't heard her voice at first or even seen her face, he connected with her soul and her precious spirit. Travis was thankful he had waited on the Lord. A small tear rolled down Travis' face and he wiped it away.

Shavon was ecstatic. Since the day Travis had proposed, she had been on cloud nine. She felt complete; not because she had a man in her life, but because God had fulfilled his promise. The proposal had been somewhat unexpected even though she knew they were in love, but they had talked about what they wanted out of life's journey and how life might be if they were married. Still, she had not anticipated his proposing to her so quickly. Others knew, but they did not want to spoil her surprise.

Travis had planned a proposal without her knowing anything about it. It was a Friday evening and Shavon was looking forward to the weekend. Everyone had gone home a little earlier than usual, but she figured it was just the start of the weekend, so she did not pay it any attention.

As she exited the building, a white limousine pulled up and asked her if she was Shavon Washington. When she answered "yes," the driver handed her a note. She opened the envelope and it read: Please join me for an early dinner. Love, Travis. P.S. Don't give the driver a hard time, just get in. Shavon laughed and the driver opened the door for her and she got in.

Once inside the limousine, there was another note and a dozen, plush red roses. The note said: Here are the twelve reasons why I love you. By the time she had reached reason number four, there were tears streaming down her face. The driver turned on the radio for her. It was a CD of "My Funny Valentine" by Miles Davis. Travis had custom made this CD because he was talking along with the music and with passion in his voice he told her how this had been the song that played the first time he held her in his arms. Shavon sat back in total astonishment; she was being wooed and it felt so very wonderful. The driver drove around for a while before stopping. He brought her to a park that was unfamiliar to her. She looked around at the beautiful surroundings.

Beside where the limousine had stopped, there was a white Clydesdale horse and buggy waiting. When she climbed up into the carriage, she found another note attached to a pink box. She opened the envelope and there was a letter that read: "If I could fly, I would fly away with you; the destination would not matter as long as I was with you. You make me feel free and with you, I want us to spread our wings and fly forever." Shavon opened up the neatly wrapped box and inside it was two tropical butterflies.

The butterflies were the most authentic butterflies she had ever seen. They amazed her as once she opened the box they flew away into the evening breeze. She was about to lose control; she couldn't take anymore and the anticipation was making her weak. She rode in the carriage to a garden in the park; it was a butterfly garden. She could see Travis standing in the distance in a white Tuxedo and he was smiling. Shavon was a basket case by now. She was crying so much the guy driving the carriage reached back and handed her a tissue. Travis briskly walked towards her and she was ready to just fall into his loving arms. She wouldn't have dreamt of anything like this in her whole life. Shavon had watched the television show, "The Wedding Story," but Travis had outdone anything like those stories she had seen.

Once he reached her, he just grabbed her and gave her the longest, tightest hug ever. She could feel their heartbeats begin to mesh and slow to the accompaniment of each other. They walked to a pavilion and there she found another guy playing the violin. Shavon felt faint; she did not feel like she was going to be able to stand up so she leaned on Travis' shoulder.

Travis read Shavon a romantic poem he had written and then said, "Shavon Washington, my love, I have been thinking about you ever since the day I met you online. You have helped me to appreciate life once again. I want to personally thank you for being so patient and such a devoted and honest friend. I have often thought about my life and how wonderful it would be if you today Shavon, would say 'yes' and marry me?"

Travis brought out a Blue Nile Signature princess cut diamond ring and knelt down on one knee. Shavon was so overcome with emotion that she hadn't heard a small crowd arrive near them in the park.

"Yes, Travis Elliott! Yes, I will marry you!"

The crowd began to clap and there was hardly a dry eye to be found. The clapping startled her and she looked around and with blurry eyes saw her parents, Tarik and Tiffany, Maria and her family, Alana and Drayton, Diane and Phillip, Pastor Dallas and First Lady Dallas and, to her great surprise, there was even Clayson, Emerald, and Jasmine. With Jasmine being there, Shavon knew God was definitely also present.

Shavon looked at the smiles on everyone's face and just knew that God had stamped his signature of approval on her and Travis' lives. She giggled to herself and thought God certainly has a sense of humor; He had sent her the 'Black Emperor' through an online Christian dating service. Shavon now understood how one could never truly understand the mysteries of God. Shavon wasn't going to spend the rest of her life trying to figure God's mysteries out. She was going to enjoy her life with Mr. Black Emperor to its utmost!

Shavon's father gave her a small peck on the cheek and said, "Today, I release my precious dove into the hands of an eagle. Shavon, I admire Travis. He's a great man. I pray that you are happy in your mind and spirit." Shavon replied with more tears in her eyes, "Daddy, I love Travis and I'm so happy. I'm so glad that I waited; I'm so glad I waited on the Lord."

CHAPTER XIII

THE WAIT IS OVER!

The time was drawing near and the wedding processional song was on its last stanza. It was time for Shavon to walk down the aisle. Shavon felt like today was the happiest day of her life, and it was. Shavon couldn't wait to see how beautiful everything would be on the inside of the church. The Word Baptist Church was a spectacular building, so the wedding adornments would only enhance it.

Shavon was shaking and her father knew she was nervous. She tried to hold back the tears, but they continued to fall like rain drops during the month of April showers. Shavon's father gave her a small peck on the cheek and said, "Today, I release my precious dove into the hands of an eagle. Shavon, I admire Travis. He's a great man.

I pray that you are happy in your mind and spirit." Shavon replied with more tears in her eyes, "Daddy, I love Travis and I'm so happy. I'm so glad that I waited; I'm so glad I waited on the Lord."

The doors of the church opened and in walked Shavon and her father. Travis looked at Shavon like he wanted to just run up to her and carry her the rest of the way down the aisle. When she finally was in front of him, he mouthed to her, "I love you, Shavon. You are so beautiful to me."

From this day forward she was going to be Mrs. Shavon Washington-Elliott. At the reception, when they gave their speeches, Travis and Shavon said, "We have only one word of advice to give all of our family and friends. 'Wait on the Lord, I say wait!'"

About the Author

Sabriena is a native of Gainesville Florida. She is the mother of Ja'kya Romea Sheppard (18) and Je'rod Harvey Sheppard (15). She currently works as a Adult Outreach Counselor for a Domestic Violence Organization. She is the founder of Total Vision Motivational Ministries. A ministry that helps to empower women to become the woman that God has called them to be. She is the author of two books, a poet, playwright and songwriter. She enjoys writing, reading and spending intimate time with God. Her passion is to reach the nations with her gift of writing.

Author's Contact Information

Sabriena Williams
P.O. Box 5973
Gainesville, FL 32627

Email Address: aninspirationaltouch@yahoo.com
Website: http://waitonthelord-isaywait.weebly.com

The author is available for book signings, women's conferences, book club meetings, cultural events, church functions, group talks, support groups, and much, much, more.

www.ingramcontent.com/pod-product-compliance
Lightning Source LLC
LaVergne TN
LVHW050634100826
845148LV00011B/1860

* 9 7 8 0 9 8 1 5 4 6 3 8 4 *